Palomino Showdown

Gold-miner Slim Harper had chased the elusive nuggets for most of his adult life, until good fortune finally smiled upon him in the Black Hills. But when he had gathered his valuable goods together, he realized that evil eyes were waiting for him to try and leave the gold fields, and return to his wife and daughter. So he sent a wire to famed lawman, Kid Palomino, to come and help him escape the notorious Tent City.

Slim waited and waited but Kid Palomino and his sidekick, Red Rivers, found that the trail from Waco to Dakota was a dangerous one. Attacked by Sioux and outlaws, the deputies had taken far longer to reach Slim than they planned. In desperation, Slim Harper set out for home on his own with ruthless killers on his tail. But could Kid Palomino reach him in time, let alone save him?

Palomino Showdown

MICHAEL D. GEORGE

A Black Horse Western

ROBERT HALE · LONDON

© Michael D. George 2004
First published in Great Britain 2004

ISBN 0 7090 7507 3

Robert Hale Limited
Clerkenwell House
Clerkenwell Green
London EC1R 0HT

Typeset by
Derek Doyle & Associates, Liverpool.
Printed and bound in Great Britain by
Antony Rowe Limited, Wiltshire

Dedicated with love, respect and gratitude to my mother and father, Olive and Denis.

PROLOGUE

Texan deputy Kid Palomino pulled back on his reins and stopped the lathered-up stallion beneath his hand-tooled saddle. He glanced over his right shoulder and watched as his friend Red Rivers eased his own buckskin pony to a halt beside him.

Neither horseman spoke as their dust-encrusted eyes surveyed the sun-weathered town that they had ridden into. If it had a name, it was known only to the startled residents who had gathered along the crumbling boardwalks in front of them.

Kid Palomino knew only too well what the eyes of their audience were looking at. It was the deputy stars pinned to his and Red's dust-caked shirts.

It was obvious to both lawmen that their presence here was not welcome. For this was a town that seemed to distrust the law. They could almost smell the hatred.

'You figurin' on staying here, strangers?' The question dripped like acid from the mouth of a tall thin man who was dressed in the fashion of a Mississippi riverboat gambler, although this place could not have been further away from the famed waterway. 'Coz we don't cotton to lawmen in these parts.'

Kid Palomino glanced along the line of men before them. They were well armed and looked as if they knew how to handle their arsenal of weaponry.

'You ain't very friendly, are you.'

'I don't have to be, sonny. This is my town!' The gambler spat at the ground.

'You reckon that I give a hoot about that?' Kid Palomino's voice was low. Almost a whisper and yet there was danger in his subdued tones.

Red Rivers tapped his spurs into the sides of his mount and drew level with his younger friend. He could sense the trouble that was brewing.

'Maybe we ought to keep on riding, Kid,' Red offered. 'I don't think these folks want our company.'

'Your pal looks a tad nervous, sonny.' The tall man grinned up at the deputy astride the palomino stallion. 'I'd heed his warning if'n I was you. Git goin'!'

Kid Palomino smiled.

'I figure my old Rhode Island Red partner don't want to fight, but I like nothing better than a good shoot-out before breakfast.'

There was a mumbling. It went up and down the line of men who faced the pair of mounted deputies.

'Big talk from a young rooster!' The man clad in gambler's attire pulled a long cigar from his breast pocket, bit the tip off it and spat it at the ground. 'I wonder if you can handle that fancy shootin'-rig you got strapped to your middle? Can you, or is it just for show?'

'You seem troubled by the presence of two tin stars in this town. Why?' the Kid asked as he pulled the gloves tight over his knuckles.

'There are some places where the law ain't welcome, boy,' the man said. His teeth gripped the cigar firmly. 'This is one of them places. I suggest you ride on.'

'Can't do that,' Kid Palomino said defiantly. 'I ain't had my breakfast yet and I'm darn hungry.'

The man dragged a match down a wooden upright and put the flame to his cigar. He sucked in on the flame until the air around his head was filled with blue aromatic smoke.

'I just knew you was the stubborn type. That's the thing about lawmen. They all think that they can do as they please just because they got themselves a tin star pinned on their vests. I warn you again, sonny. Ride on or you'll regret it!'

'All we want is some grub and fresh water,' Red Rivers piped up. 'There ain't no call for any bloodshed.'

The gambler nodded as he sucked on the cigar and stared at the square-jawed Kid Palomino. He had heard of a young lawman who rode a magnificent palomino stallion. A man who was said to be one of the fastest draws in Texas. Until now, he had thought the stories were just tall tales. Now he was beginning to realize that the man actually existed. And if he existed, then some of the stories about his gun skills might just be true as well.

'What they call you, sonny?' The man asked through a cloud of smoke.

'Kid Palomino!'

The gambler felt a bead of sweat trickle from his hat-band and trail down his face. Even the name chilled him.

'I figured as much.' The voice had lost its sharp edge as the man chewed on the black-leafed cigar.

'Who in tarnation is Kid Palomino, Reno?' one of the other men asked the gambler.

'Hush up.'

'You heard of me?' the Kid asked.

'I heard of you, Kid!'

Palomino could sense that the gambler was now less eager to start a fight.

'Nothing good, I'll wager.'

Reno allowed the acrid smoke to fill his lungs.

'What you doin' in my town? You huntin' bounty?'

'Nope. We ain't bounty hunters. We're just passing through. Just passing through,' Palomino replied.

The gambler sighed heavily as he turned and shook his head at the men who did his bidding.

'Best let this pair grab themselves some vittles and fresh water, boys,' Reno told them.

There was a look of astonishment on every face. They had never seen their leader back down before and it troubled them.

'What?' the nearest of the gunmen asked. 'Are you sure about that, Reno? We can take them for sure!'

'That hoss of his must be worth hundreds, Reno!'

another of his men gestured. 'We just gonna do nothin'?'

'Nothin' at all!' The gambler placed the cigar between his teeth and nodded for the final time before walking into the saloon behind them.

Slowly, the brooding gunmen followed their leader into the dark interior of the decaying wooden building. They knew better than argue with the tall gambler. If he was not willing to draw down on someone, there had to be a very good reason. For Reno was many things, but a coward was not one of them.

The trail had been long and hard. For more than two months the pair of riders had headed further and further north. Now they were in a land that neither of them knew or recognized, but they had continued forging ahead relentlessly, as if drawn by an invisible force.

This town was just one more spot on the crude map that Kid Palomino had in his saddle-bags: another stepping-stone that would bring them closer to their eventual goal. Both riders had journeyed to many places during the years that they had travelled and worked together, but never had they embarked on a quest like this one.

This journey was different.

This time they were neither drifting nor riding to a place where their skills as lawmen were required. The handsome Kid Palomino had received a wire back in Waco. He had been so concerned by it that he immediately decided to head north to seek out its author. His partner Red Rivers had saddled up without question and decided to hit the trail with him. For, wherever Kid Palomino led, Red followed.

'You figure this town is safe, Kid?' Red asked his silent companion as his eyes darted around the street of bleached wooden buildings. 'These varmints don't want us here and I don't want to have a bullet finding my back.'

Kid Palomino rested the palm of his left hand on the silver saddle horn and then slowly dismounted. He wrapped the reins around the hitching rail and allowed his horse to drink from the full trough. He shared his friend's concerns but was not willing to show it. The men who hung around the gambler were the sort who preyed upon any sign of weakness. He had to give the appearance of strength. He knew it was their only insurance against being backshot.

'You listening to me, Palomino?' Red asked.

'Did you catch the name of the tall thin dude dressed as a gambler, Red?' Palomino looked straight at his pal.

'The fat man called him Reno,' Red Rivers replied as he too slid from his saddle. 'Why?'

'Reno! Yeah, that was it.' Palomino repeated the name. 'No wonder he's a mite nervous of seeing two deputies riding in here.'

'Is he wanted?' Red enquired as he tied his own reins to the hitching rail.

Palomino rubbed his dry mouth.

'You bet! Johnny Reno's worth a lot of money dead or alive, if my memory serves me correctly.'

Red stepped up on to the boardwalk beside his pal.

'Is he why we done rode a hundred or so miles, Kid?'

'Nope. This ain't where we're headed.' The Kid pointed down the street at a sun-bleached sign. 'Look, Red. A café. Let's go get us some breakfast and then head out of here.'

Red shrugged. 'I don't know why I follow you into these kinda places, Kid. Am I loco?'

'Yep! That's why I like you!'

The two men walked along the creaking boards. Their spurs rang out a tune in the morning sun which they knew was attracting many unseen eyes from the surrounding buildings. Window drapes moved from almost every house and storefront.

'I don't like this place, Kid,' Red admitted. 'I got me a darn bad feeling about this town.'

Palomino turned the door-handle and entered.

'It ain't the town that you have to be wary of, Red. It's the gunmen who do Reno's bidding.'

'You figure that they'll start something?'

Palomino removed his pale Stetson and dropped it on to a chair before sitting down with his back to the wall.

'I sure hope they don't, Red. I don't wanna waste time here shooting it out with no outlaws. I have better things to do with my time.'

Red Rivers stared at his friend as he too sat down with his back to the wall. What could have caused Kid Palomino to be like this? Why was he so desperate to reach the sender of that unknown message?

At last the bearded red-haired man could stand it no longer.

'Where are we headed, Kid?'

'North, Red,' Palomino replied, removing his gloves and dropping them into his upturned hat. 'I told you before that we're headed north.'

Red Rivers gave a huge frustrated sigh and rubbed his face with the tails of his bandanna.

'To where exactly?'

Kid Palomino was staring at the window as he replied: 'You'll find out when we get there.'

'C'mon, *amigo*. What's the fuss all about?'

'You'll see.'

'I'm getting a tad worried, Kid,' Red confessed.

'You ain't alone. I'm a tad troubled myself.' Kid Palomino watched as the elderly cook moved from his hot cooking range to their table. 'Ham and eggs, please.'

The cook nodded gratefully.

'Coffee?'

'Yep. A pot of coffee and a bowl of sugar.' The Kid smiled and watched the old man move back to his cooking range.

'And apple-pie, old-timer,' Red added loudly.

'Both of you want pie?' the cook asked.

'Yep.' The Kid nodded.

'Five minutes.'

'That'll be just fine.' Palomino smiled.

'I ain't never questioned you before, Kid,' Red said. 'I always let you do the thinkin' coz you've

14

always been a lot better at it than me, but I'm getting worried. Where are we headed?'

Palomino rubbed the dust off his chin and pointed at the window.

'We got other things to worry about at the moment, Red. Look!'

Red Rivers looked up at the grubby windowpanes. A few of the men who had been gathered around the gambler called Reno were now opposite the small café. They stood watching.

'I don't think they believed you when you said that we was just passing through here, Kid.'

'I know. They have probably all got sizeable bounties on their heads and they figure that we're here to claim them. But I think we're safe as long as we stay in here.'

'Then I'm gonna eat darn slow,' Red said, scratching his beard. 'Them varmints are gonna die of old age before I goes out in that street again.'

Kid Palomino smiled as he continued watching the men who were staring at the small building.

'I wonder if Johnny Reno knows that a few of his boys are getting ambitious, Red?'

'Maybe he sent them just to keep an eye on us.'

Kid Palomino silently pulled both his guns from their holsters and laid them on top of the table.

ONE

The two lawmen finished off their meals and drank the last of the coffee. Yet neither man had concentrated fully on what the elderly cook had placed before them. They only had eyes for the three well-armed men who waited patiently in the shadows for them to come out again into the street.

Then they saw another man joining the trio. He too was well laden down with guns and rifle.

The Kid's mind raced as he tried to make sense of the situation they found themselves in. Were these men waiting to shoot it out with him and Red or were they simply waiting to get a chance at placing well-aimed bullets in their backs as he and his partner made their way back to their waiting horses?

Perhaps they were simply watching to ensure that the pair of lawmen did exactly as they said. Eat, water their horses and themselves and ride on out.

Palomino rose to his feet. He dropped a few coins on the table and then picked up his hat. He pulled the gloves out of its crown and tucked them into his gunbelt before placing the Stetson back on to his head.

'Ever seen vultures perched on the branch of a tree, Red?'

'What?'

'They just sit and wait for something to die,' the Kid said as he plucked his Colts up and dropped them into his holsters. He then moved away from the table and stood in the centre of the room. 'Vultures have got a lot of patience. I wonder if them gunmen are patient?'

'They're Reno's boys, gents,' the cook said from behind his large wooden counter. 'I seen them like this before. They are just waiting for you to go back out in the street and then they'll back-shoot you both.'

'Back-shooters?' Red gulped, got to his feet and dragged his hat down over his thinning hair. 'I knew they was back-shooters, Kid.'

'Yep.' The cook sniffed. 'Reno has a lot of the critters on his payroll.'

Red moved next to his taller friend.

'You hear the old man, Kid?'

'I heard!' Palomino answered.

'I could let you use the back door if you reckon you can get to your horses.' The cook was taking a risk by warning his two customers and they both knew it.

'C'mon, Kid. Let's cut out through the back like the old man said.' Red flipped the safety loop off his gun and teased it in the holster.

'Nope. I'm going out the same way as I came in,' Palomino said.

'But why?' Red was nervous. Real nervous.

'If we use the back door, they might figure that the cook warned us. That sort would take pleasure in teaching him a lesson.' The Kid loosened his pair of matched Colts in their holsters and rested his palms on their ivory grips. 'No. I'm going out the front door and facing them.'

'But them critters is back-shooters!'

'Come on, Red.' Kid Palomino walked slowly to the door and opened it. He squinted into the bright sunlight. 'Let's get back to our horses and ride out of here.'

Red kept his hand on the grip of his pistol and reluctantly followed Palomino out on to the board-walk.

'You look ahead and I'll keep an eye on what's back of us!'

The two men walked slowly back along the dry creaking boardwalk with their hands resting on their guns. Red watched as the four men behind them began trailing their every step.

'They're coming on after us, Kid.'

'Thought they would,' Palomino replied. 'I can't see nobody ahead of us yet.'

As the deputies reached the water trough they slipped under the necks of their drinking mounts and untied the knots of their reins from the hitching pole.

'The four men behind us have stopped walking,

Kid,' Red informed his partner as they gathered up the reins. They moved to their horses' sides and gripped the saddle horns with their left hands whilst keeping their gun hands on the grips of their Colts.

'Mount up, Red,' Kid Palomino ordered.

Both men raised their left legs and slipped their pointed boots into the stirrups. They eased themselves up on to their saddles, then nudged their mounts away from the trough.

Johnny Reno stepped out into the sunshine from the dark interior of the saloon, holding on to the lapels of his frock coat. He stared up at the two riders with venomous eyes. It reminded both lawmen of a rattler that was ready to strike.

'Call your men off, Reno!' Kid Palomino snarled across the distance between them. 'Call them off and we'll ride on out as promised.'

'And if'n I don't?' Reno sneered.

Kid Palomino drew the Colt from his right holster and aimed at the gambler. 'Then my first bullet will go straight through your head!'

'How come you ain't interested in me or my men, Kid?' Reno asked defiantly. 'Where you headed and why are you headed there?'

Palomino cocked the hammer of the Colt.

'Call them off, Reno!'

Reno glanced at the four men standing in the middle of the street with their hands on their guns. They were ready for a signal to slap leather. A signal that the gambler was unwilling to make.

'Let 'em go, boys!' Reno called out. 'We don't

want to bring ourselves bad luck by killing two lawmen.'

The four gunmen obeyed without question and walked to the side of the gambler who was still staring down the barrel of the Colt .45 in Kid Palomino's hand.

'Don't come back, Kid!' Reno growled.

'I don't intend coming back here, Reno.' Palomino stood in his stirrups, hauled his mount's head to his left and whipped the long reins across its shoulders. The stallion thundered down the dusty street with Red Rivers a few yards behind him on his buckskin. The sound of the horses' hoofs echoed around the wooden buildings.

Neither horsemen looked back.

'We could have killed them easy, boss!' one of the gunman drawled angrily.

'Yeah, they wouldn't have stood a chance!' another added.

'Sure you could have, boys!' Reno agreed. 'The problem is he would have blown my brains out a split second before your guns left their holsters.'

'Yeah, he did kinda draw that hogleg fast!' One of the gunmen nodded.

Johnny Reno pulled another long cigar from his breast pocket, bit off its tip and spat it at the ground.

'Get our horses, Luke!' Johnny Reno commanded quietly with a wave of his hand.

'What for?'

'We're gonna trail Kid Palomino, you fool.' Reno struck a match and cupped its flame before guiding it to the end of the long black cigar.

'We is gonna trail them? Why?' the fat gunman asked. Reno puffed for a few moments as his eyes watched the dust settling along the length of the empty street. Smoke billowed from the gambler's dry, narrow lips as he continued to stare down the long street.

'I figure that Kid Palomino don't back away from a fight that easy unless he has something more profitable in mind. Wherever he's going, it must be worth a lot of money to him and his sidekick.'

'Ain't he honest?' the fat gunman asked curiously. 'I thought that the stories about him said he was real honest.'

'Yeah! I heard that too, Reno!' Luke agreed.

'I never met a lawman who was honest, *amigos*!' Reno grinned. 'Get our horses! We got us some trailing to do!'

TWO

For hours the pair of lawmen had ridden continu-
ously north until the ferocious sun had given way to
the bone-chilling eventuality of night. The trail
wound its way up through a million trees and toward
the summit of an unnamed mountain peak. As the
cold slowly gnawed its way into the bones of the
Texans, they had decided to make camp for the
night.

Flames from the raging camp-fire licked at the
night sky as Kid Palomino sat against his saddle on
the soft ground. He had watched as Red piled more
and more dry kindling on to the already roaring fire.

'You reckon you got enough wood on that fire,
Red?'

'I'm cold, Kid!' the older man complained.

'Then do up the buttons on your coat.'

Red dropped more wood into the centre of the
flames.

'It ain't natural to button a coat all the way up,
Palomino.'

'I know. But this ain't Texas.' The Kid grinned. 'A man could freeze to death in these parts.'

'I don't know why I tag along with you,' Red grumbled. 'It always leads to trouble. Well? Don't it?'

'Yep!' Kid Palomino conceded.

There was no moon above them and countless stars sparkled as if warning of the night frost yet to come. The older deputy stared heavenward and then looked down at his grinning pal.

'More coffee, Kid?' Red asked as he crouched down and allowed his thin frame to absorb the heat.

Palomino nodded and held out the tin cup. He watched as the older man wrapped a well-worn rag around his hand, hoisted the small blackened coffee pot from out of the fire's embers and poured the last of its dark brew into the tin cup.

'I figure that you've got enough wood on that fire to last the whole night, Red.' The Kid smiled as his keen eyes surveyed the surrounding trees as the flickering light danced across their tall straight trunks.

'I ain't finished yet.'

The Kid nodded. 'You could be right. This sure ain't Texas weather.'

'I ain't gonna freeze tonight!' Red replied as he searched his saddle-bags for some hardtack. 'I reckon we're half-way up this mountain and I don't cotton to mountains.'

'Why not?'

'Coz mountains usually got snow on the tops of them.' Red shivered as he thought about his words. 'And no Texan likes snow. It just ain't natural.'

Kid Palomino sipped at his coffee and thought about the telegram in his pocket. He had not told Red a thing about its contents and yet his loyal friend had still ridden with him into the unknown.

'Reckon it's time I showed you the message I received at Waco, Red.' Palomino sighed. 'You've earned the right to see why I'm so all-fired up.'

Red sat down and accepted the piece of paper that Palomino drew from the breast pocket of his jacket. He carefully unfolded it and tilted it so that the light of the flames would enable him to read its brief contents.

TO KID PALOMINO. SHERIFF'S OFFICE. WACO. TEXAS. HAVE STRUCK IT LUCKY. BUT I NEED HELP TO GET BACK TO EDITH AND SOPHIE WITH GOODS. SOME FOLKS HERE WANT TO STOP ME. COME AT ONCE TO THE ANGEL HOTEL, TENT CITY, DAKOTA. SLIM.

'Well?'

'Who in tarnation is this Slim character?' Red Rivers scratched his beard as he tried to work out the brief telegraph message. 'And what does it mean?'

'Slim is one of them men who has spent most of his grown life searching for gold, Red,' Kid Palomino answered. 'By the tone of that wire, I think he must have finally hit paydirt. But Slim being Slim, he's attracted the attention of someone who wants to take his newly found wealth off him. That's why I've been so secretive.'

Red returned the paper to his friend.

'I never heard you speak of anyone called Slim before, Palomino.'

'I got my reasons,' The Kid said into the tin cup. 'But he needs my help by the sound of it.'

'Our help, Kid!' Red corrected.

The Kid smiled.

'I knew that you'd not let me down.'

Red gazed into the hypnotic flames of the fire.

'Who are Edith and Sophie?'

'His wife and daughter. I never met them, but I know that they live at Cooper's City.' Palomino nursed the cup in his hands and stared all around their campsite for the umpteenth time. He was nervous.

For the first time since leaving Waco, he was nervous.

'What's wrong, Kid?' Red asked. 'You look darn edgy.'

Palomino rested the empty cup on the sand.

'I got me a feeling that we ain't alone in this forest.'

Red looked all around them at the trees which were bathed in the dancing light of his roaring fire.

'There are always critters in places like this, Kid. Relax and get some shut-eye. You'll feel a lot better in the morning.'

'Yeah.' Kid Palomino rose to his feet. 'I guess that you're right. I think that I let Johnny Reno and his vermin spook me a tad earlier.'

'So that's why you didn't even try to arrest him!' Red nodded knowingly. 'You couldn't waste the time

26

taking Reno all the way back to civilization. Could you?'

'Yep. You're right!' the Kid agreed. 'It really made me angry having to back down from him and his men. But I just have to try and reach Slim as soon as possible. He'll get himself killed for sure otherwise!'

'I know the sort.'

'Don't look at me that way, Red.' The Kid grinned, 'I don't get into many fixes, do I?'

'Ain't for me to point no fingers.' Red smiled and then got up. He dusted himself down before picking up more logs and dropping them into the heart of the blazing fire. 'Let's check the horses and get us some sleep. You're worn out.'

The Kid agreed.

'You're right, Red. I'm just tired.'

Both men walked to their mounts and checked that they were still secured to the running line they had strung between two trees.

'Easy, Nugget!' the Kid whispered into the ear of his prized palomino stallion as he ran a hand along its neck. 'Our journey is almost done. Then I'll let them pamper you at the best livery stable in Tent City.'

'Where is this Tent City, Kid?' Red asked. 'I ain't heard of it before.'

'It's one of them gold towns up in the Black Hills,' Palomino replied.

Red moved closer to his pal.

'The Black Hills, you say?'

'Yep! Why?'

Red's eyes were much wider as he repeated the name again.

'The Black Hills! Ain't that Injun country?'

Kid Palomino smiled and rested a hand on Red's shoulder.

'There ain't nothing to fret about, Red. They reckon it's darn peaceful there since Custer opened up the territory.'

Red Rivers bent down, picked up another pile of kindling and tossed it into the fire. The flames grew higher and the heat more intense.

'I'll be honest with you, Kid,' Red started. 'I want you to let me know when we reach the Injun country. OK?'

'I hate to tell you this, Red.'

'Tell me what, Kid?'

'We've been in Indian country for the last couple of days.'

Red removed his hat and ran his fingers over his thinning red hair. He gulped.

'But I ain't exactly fixed for scalpin', Kid.'

Suddenly the sound of a breaking branch caused both men's attention to be drawn to their left. Kid Palomino placed a hand on Red's sleeve as he drew one of his Colts.

'Keep talkin', Red.'

Before Red could reply, he noticed that his younger friend had disappeared into the under-growth behind them. He gulped and then started mumbling loudly to himself.

28

THREE

The forest was pitch black beyond the range of the flickering camp-fire's dancing light. Kid Palomino held on to one of his prized matched Colts as he slowly descended between the tall pine trees. He moved to where he and his nervous partner had heard the sound of a branch being broken. Whoever or whatever had stepped on the fragile length of wood was no longer anywhere to be seen. The Kid knelt and touched the disturbed ground with his gloved left hand, but it was too dark to see anything.

For a few moments the deputy listened to the sounds of the forest around him. His mind raced as he wondered whether their camp had attracted either a curious animal or perhaps a deadly foe.

He knew that there were still Indians in this land. Indians who had once been forced out by the intrusion of the gold-miners and their army escorts.

Sweat trickled down the Kid's face as he gradually rose up again to his full height and stared around him into the darkness.

He was scared!

If their camp-fire had lured an Indian, it was probably a good bet that he and Red would end up targets during the long night.

Palomino rubbed his dry mouth with his gloved fingers and slowly made his way downhill through the trees. He knew that there was a lot of game in this almost uncharted land and hoped that he might see a mountain lion or even a deer as he circled the area around his and Red's camp.

Then, as he forced his way through the brush between two trees, he spotted a huge black mass crouched at the foot of a tree-trunk.

Swallowing hard, the Kid eased his way closer and then stopped. He screwed up his eyes desperately trying to focus on the object.

Whatever it was, it was alive!

Palomino tried to move sideways across the ground as quietly as he could. With every step, the sound of his own heart pounding inside his chest seemed to grow louder.

The shape moved!

The Kid stopped and gripped his gun tightly in his right hand. Its barrel was trained on the shape.

The it moved again!

The Kid felt himself shaking as he managed to make out that the dark shadowy vision was rising.

It was a bear!

The low growl told Palomino that his presence had been noted by the keen instincts of the animal. He leaned against the trunk of a tree, slowly drew his second Colt from its holster and cocked its hammer.

Now both barrels were aimed at the huge bear!

He wondered if he could stop such a massive animal with the bullets in his weapons.

The bear was big. But was it also fast? He had never seen one of these creatures at close quarters before, but had been told that they could move faster than a man could blink if they chose to attack.

More sweat traced its way down the Kid's face.

Again, he tried to keep the dark shape of the animal in focus as it moved away from the tree. The low growl chilled Palomino to the bone. It was like a warning that he knew he must heed.

Then the bear rose up on its back legs!

The Kid could hardly believe the size of the creature. It had to be nearly eight feet in height. Its long claws glinted in what light there was as the bear gave out a spine-chilling roar.

It took every ounce of the deputy's courage not to squeeze the triggers of his matched Colts. He stood defiantly facing the animal that was only a matter of twelve feet from him.

Their eyes met across the short distance between them.

Without warning, the bear dropped back down on to all fours, snorted and turned away from him. Before the Kid had time to catch his breath, the animal had run off into the protection of the blackness.

Kid Palomino felt himself sighing in relief. He had no way of knowing whether he would have survived an attack by the bear even if he had managed to empty both his guns into the creature.

He doubted it though. There were some things that even bullets could not stop.

As he slid one of his guns back into its holster, he noticed something else through the trees. Kid Palomino walked to where the huge bear had been standing only a few seconds earlier, parted some overhanging branches and gazed down the steep slope.

A camp-fire could easily be seen in the darkness of the forested ground below him.

Kid Palomino sighed heavily.

It was obvious that he and Red were being trailed.

Red Rivers continued to move around the camp-fire, feeding kindling on to its flames. His eyes darted to every shadow that moved in the flickering light against the trees. Sweat ran freely down his bearded face, but it was not the heat of the fire that caused it.

It was the fear of the unknown.

Kid Palomino had vanished into the darkness between the trees more than five minutes earlier and Red was beginning to wonder whether he would ever see his impetuous partner again.

They had both heard the unmistakable sound of a branch being broken by someone or something step-ping on to it. As usual, the Kid had acted instinctively and gone to investigate who or what had been attracted to their camp.

'Darn fool!' Red repeated over and over again as

he stooped and plucked at the ground for scraps of wood. 'Why do you always have to go off half-cocked like this?'

The toothless mouth of the red-haired deputy was getting dryer with every passing heartbeat. He knew that this land was dangerous. Red could sense it in every sinew of his body.

Then a sudden noise behind him made Red almost jump out of his skin.

He slapped leather, hauled his Colt from its holster and swung around. His thumb cocked the hammer until it locked fully. He aimed straight at where he had heard the nerve-breaking sound.

'You better come on out or I'll start shooting!' Red heard himself shout.

'Easy, partner!' Palomino's voice called out. 'I don't want to eat your lead. Holster that iron before you shoot one of us.'

Every muscle in Red's body was shaking as he released the hammer of his gun and then lowered its barrel.

'Kid?'

'You OK, Red?' Kid Palomino walked out into the light and up to his friend. 'You can start breathing again.'

Red Rivers inhaled deeply and then slid his gun back into its holster.

'What you trying to do, Kid?' he ranted. 'Give me heart failure? I thought you was an Injun or maybe a puma. What you want to go scaring me for?'

'How come you're so skittish?' Kid Palomino

plucked his bedroll up off the ground and started to undo the leather laces.

'What made the noise out there?' Red asked, pointing at the trees. 'You know, the reason that you went off into the woods?'

Kid Palomino tossed his head back.

'Oh yeah.'

'Well?'

Palomino shook the bedroll loose and then draped it across the ground near his horse's hoofs.

'I didn't find anything.'

'Nothing?' Red gasped.

'Nope. Not a darn thing.' The Kid shrugged and then turned his head to look at his friend. 'Except one really big bear, that is.'

'A bear?' Red was now even more nervous.

'Yep. A big one. He looked at me and I looked at him and then he decided to take himself a walk.' The Kid grinned. 'For a moment there I thought that I was a goner!'

Red swallowed hard. 'Are there any Injuns up here? Are there, Kid?'

Kid Palomino removed his Stetson and dropped it down on to his saddle at the top of his bedroll.

'I'm not too sure.'

Red watched as the kid knelt down and removed his hand-tooled gunbelt. Then he lay down on his back with his head against the saddle.

'I reckon that there still has to be some Sioux out there someplace, Kid. Custer couldn't have scared the whole tribe out of these forests.'

'I was thinking the same thing, Red.' The Kid smiled as he tucked his arms behind his head and stared into the flames.

'The fire ought to keep animals at bay though,' Red said in a tone that seemed to indicate that he was not too certain about the statement.

'I did find out one thing though.' Palomino sighed and closed his eyes.

Red dropped on to his knees beside Palomino and shook his pal hard.

'What did you find out? C'mon, Kid. Don't go keeping no secrets from me.'

'We ain't alone on this mountain,' the Kid muttered.

'Huh?'

Palomino opened one eye and looked straight at the older deputy.

'I made my way a couple of hundred yards down the hill before I met the bear. Then I saw something. I figure that someone is trailing us. I could see a camp-fire licking up through the trees.'

Red rubbed the sweat off his brow with his shirt sleeve.

'How far behind us?'

'A couple of miles,' came the reply.

The red-haired deputy scratched his beard thoughtfully.

'Could they creep up on us during the night? I don't reckon I'd like to wake up and find that some critter had killed me in my sleep.'

Palomino closed his eye again and sighed heavily.

'I doubt they'll try and catch up with us, Red. I figure that whoever it is following us don't want to catch us. They're just trying to find out where we're headed and why.'

'But nobody knows that we headed this way!'

'Sure they do!' Palomino sighed.

'They do?' Red Rivers looked puzzled as he grabbed hold of his own bedroll and started to untie its leather laces.

'Think about it!'

Red snapped his fingers.

'Johnny Reno!'

'Yep! Johnny Reno!' the Kid agreed.

FOUR

Tent City was well named. The heavy canvas covering the crude wooden-framed structures stretched off in all directions in the flat valley between two imposing pine-tree-clad hills. At the foot of the infamous Black Hills the 7th Cavalry had set up camp in order to protect the scores of gold prospectors and the thousands of human parasites that always followed them.

Only one building had been constructed as if it were meant to last and that was part saloon and part house of ill repute. The two-storey edifice dominated everything else in Tent City for good reason. Considering the sheer volume of trade the wood-panelled structure had to cope with, it had to be well built.

The acrid smell that lingered in, around and over Tent City was something that could have kept the Indians at bay with or without the presence of the hundreds of cavalrymen.

Yet only strangers seemed to notice the aroma.

The residents of Tent City either did not or could not notice anything unpleasant on the warm air.

They had other things on their minds. The men with the picks and gold pans were too preoccupied in digging out the golden ore from the surrounding hills or panning from the streams and rivers. The people who had set up their businesses to milk the precious yellow nuggets and dust from the gold prospectors could only smell the profits to be made in this remote landscape.

Tent City had everything men either needed or wanted. The traders could sell them anything. From food, liquor and boiled candy to the company of willing females. All at a price. A very high price.

The army turned a blind eye to nearly everything that went on within the boundaries of the sea of tents. On a few occasions they ventured into Tent City to try to give the impression that they were in control. But in truth, there was little actual law in this booming settlement.

For the cavalry, their presence was simply a way of taking another chunk of land from the native tribes who legally owned something that Washington regretted having given to them.

The Black Hills had been thought worthless only a decade earlier. Then gold had been discovered there. Gold that made the treaties worthless.

There was no real law in this place.

For men worked harder when not restricted by laws.

Gold was already being shipped out in vast

volumes and there was an awful lot more still lying in the once unspoiled soil. There were no losers here, except the rightful owners of the land. Yet their voices would never be heard above the sound of those who had invaded the foothills.

Even though Tent City had only existed for a matter of months, it had already started to fall into the trap that all such places did.

The strong and evil had managed to exert their power over the less able. Gangs had followed the supply wagons into the remote hills knowing that there were rich pickings to be had.

Hooper Blake had brought his ruthless band of killers into the sprawling ocean of canvas. He had nothing to sell, but he was already rich. For Hooper Blake knew how to extort the wealth of others by well-practised methods. He had a way of making others pay for the privilege of being allowed to remain alive.

When others had ridden into Tent City with tools and goods, Blake had arrived with six heavily armed outriders. Men who were skilled in only one trade.

Killing!

The broad-shouldered gunfighter knew how to frighten more honest souls into parting with a percentage of their gold. His cruel smile and deep-set eyes could scare even the strongest of men. Those who did not comply found that he and his men could use their weaponry.

A dozen men lay in shallow graves as testament to that simple fact. Hooper Blake always got what he wanted and there was no one capable of stopping him.

The Angel Hotel was big as tents go. It had started off as a single tent and grown to over 200 feet square. One wooden frame was joined to another, all were covered in the same sort of heavy canvas that dominated the entire valley. It vainly tried to live up to its impressive name, but would never be more than a series of tents joined together.

Hooper Blake had taken over nearly half its rooms for himself and his gunmen. He paid no rent after coming to an arrangement with Fred Smith, the owner of the Angel. Nobody knew exactly what the arrangement was but most thought that allowing Smith to remain alive had some part in it.

A few of the other hotel guests were men who had managed to make their fortune quickly. They remained in the hotel until they were able to get passage back to civilization.

Blake knew them all and they knew that they were all living on borrowed time. For to escape this place with anything was almost impossible.

Slim Harper was a man who had wasted his entire life chasing the mother lode. He had travelled from one gold-strike to another trying to get his hands on the precious golden ore. This time he had been lucky and had been allocated a small twenty-foot-square scrap of land by the army.

To his surprise and delight it was rich in nuggets of gold.

Within twelve weeks he had managed to fill three

chests with the golden rocks. He had a fortune at his fingertips and decided that this time he would quit before it disappeared into the hands of the businesses within Tent City. The inflated prices could strip even the largest of gold strikes and Slim knew it. He sold his small claim for a few dollars and then brought the three chests to the Angel Hotel. He had intended to buy a wagon and make his way back to his wife and daughter but then became aware of Hooper Blake and his henchmen.

The trail that led out from the Black Hills was a lonely and dangerous one. Stories of others trying to escape this place with their gold had already circulated around the city of tents.

Slim knew that he had to get out of here before Hooper Blake decided to take the gold from him.

The last two stagecoaches had been attacked and robbed and yet the army still would not give it an escort out of the gold-fields.

Slim Harper knew that he had taken a risk in sending a telegraph message to Kid Palomino, but it was the only way he could see of managing to return to his small family with his fortune intact.

So far Slim had been able to keep away from Hooper Blake and the men he controlled. The three gold-filled chests were hidden in a corner of the small canvas-walled room beneath unwashed work-clothes, but Slim knew that it was only a matter of time before Blake would find out.

The morning air was crisp as Slim walked out on to the wooden boardwalks and studied the muddy streets. He had managed to remain in the Angel Hotel, apparently unnoticed by Blake, for far longer than any of the other prospectors.

He knew that time was running out.

The smoke from the tent directly opposite him told him that bacon was being fried up for breakfast. His eyes moved away from the crude wooden sign with CAFÉ painted upon it. He checked the battered silver watch in his vest pocket. It was nearly eight and Tent City was already busy.

He stepped down into the mud and made his way across the wide street. Slim negotiated his way into the tent and waved at the man cooking the bacon on a large cast-iron range.

The man, who looked part Chinese, nodded and peeled two large rashers of bacon off a metal plate.

The sound of it hitting the hot fat filled the air.

Through the open canvas flap of the tent he saw the men opposite him leaving the Angel. They were Hooper Blake and three of his hired guns.

Slim felt a cold shiver trace his spine as they all stepped down into the street and began walking towards the café.

'Lookee like trouble, Mister Slim!' the cook said.

'Yep. Sure does, *amigo*!' Slim agreed.

FIVE

Hooper Blake stepped up on to the boardwalk and started to scrape the thick mud from his boots with the sharp stiletto knife he kept in the deep right-hand pocket of his knee-length leather jacket.

Bronson, Franks and Weaver stood beside their cursing leader, silently looking into the smoke-filled café tent. None of them looked hungry. Their eyes were focused on the seated Slim who nervously rested the palm of his right hand upon the grip of his brand new Colt .45.

'He's in there, Hoop!' Bronson spat a lump of black goo at the muddy boards and pointed.

'I know, Bronson!' Blake responded before cleaning the blade of his deadly knife on his sleeve. 'That's why I come across the street.'

The gunman spat again and bit off another chunk of chewing-tobacco.

'He looks like a scared rabbit.' Weaver laughed.

'Good!' Blake said. He ducked and entered the tent.

Slim felt his spine go wet as he leaned back against the hardback chair. He watched as the four men approached his table and knew that they wanted him.

'Howdy, gents,' Slim said as Blake sat down opposite him.

'Keep that gun in its holster, Harper,' Blake ordered in a hushed tone. 'You might just live a tad longer.'

Slim kept his hand on the gun handle.

'I don't want any trouble, Blake.'

Hooper Blake nodded to his men.

'What you want and what you get don't worry us none.'

Slim tried to keep aware of the men who were moving around him. It was impossible.

'You sure can sweat, Harper!' Blake noted as he toyed with the long lethal blade of his knife. 'I like to see a man sweat coz it means he's taking me seriously. You keep on sweating, Harper.'

Slim tried to force a smile but his face seemed to be frozen with fear. He kept stroking the grip of his gun as the three henchmen moved behind him.

'What's all this about?'

Blake grinned. It was the most terrifying grin that Slim had ever witnessed.

'You'll never make a poker-player. You thought that me and my boys hadn't noticed you. You were wrong. I've had my eye on you for quite some time.'

'Why should you notice me, Blake?' Slim asked.

'I think we both know the answer to that question.'

44

Hooper Blake's voice was low and considered. He had done this countless times before and had become an expert in making sure that he scared his opponents half to death before actually doing anything more physical.

'I reckon you must have me confused with someone else, *amigo*.' Slim heard his own words drip from his dry lips and yet knew that neither of these men were convinced by his pathetic attempt to bluff them.

Blake's eyebrow rose. 'You've disappointed me. I've been waiting for you to try and get out of Tent City with all that gold. The trouble is you've not moved an inch.'

'Why should I?'

Blake looked at the steel knife-blade between his fingers. It was the look of a man who liked to use the cold steel.

'I want you to run because you have something that belongs to me, Harper.'

'I ain't got nothing that belongs to you, Blake.'

'What about them three boxes of gold ore in your room?'

Slim felt as if he were drowning in his own sweat.

'I think that belongs to me.'

Blake slowly shook his head.

'It's mine, Harper!'

Slim went to move forward but the hands of the three men behind him grabbed at his shoulders and head. He was pulled violently back down on to his seat.

'I dug that gold out of the ground with my bare

45

hands! I ain't gonna give it away to no gunslingers.'

'So what?'

'You can't take my gold!' Slim shouted angrily.

'Hoop can do anything he likes!' Franks growled into the ear of the terrified and confused man.

Blake rose and began using the deadly knife-tip to pluck dirt from beneath his fingernails.

'I'd take it off you right now, but the cavalry might get a tad interested in me and my boys if I did. We don't wanna give them soldiers any call to come nosing around here. Far better if folks lose their money out on the open trail.'

Slim Harper knew that his worst fears had become a reality. Blake wanted the small fortune that Slim had accumulated, for himself.

'I don't think you need my gold. I've heard that you've already managed to steal a good share of the nuggets in Tent City.'

Blake ignored the words of the man he faced.

'I'll expect you to try and ride out of Tent City with your gold, Harper.' Blake smiled again. 'Then me and the boys will trail you. I figure that there's a chance that you might make it out of the Black Hills, but I kinda doubt it.'

'You don't frighten me!' Slim snapped as the three gunmen moved away from him and out on to the boardwalk. He watched as the three looked into the café at their leader.

Hooper Blake slipped the knife into his jacket pocket and turned to follow his men.

'Run, rabbit! Run!' Blake said as he slowly walked

past the cook and out into the street.

'What if I stay in town?' Slim asked. 'Does that mean that you'd leave me and my goods alone? Maybe you're scared of the army!'

Blake looked over his shoulder. His stare said it all.

'Nope! You'll end up dead either way, Harper. I just don't like the thought of them soldier boys coming in here asking dumb questions. But if they do, I'll have to live with it.'

Slim was shaking as the plate of fried bacon was placed before him. He nodded at the cook and watched the outlaws returning across the street to the Angel Hotel.

'Men very bad!' The cook said.

'Yep!' Slim agreed. 'Do you know anyone who'll sell me a buckboard or wagon?'

The cook shrugged.

'You run from men, Mister Slim?'

'I'm sure gonna try.'

b

SIX

Kid Palomino reined in his magnificent stallion and stood in his stirrups as his pal caught up with him atop the buckskin quarter horse. The dust from the hoofs of both horses drifted off the high ridge and out into the thin morning air.

'What's wrong, Kid?' Red asked, gathering up his reins and staring down the tree-lined trail.

The Kid pointed.

'See that dust?'

Red squinted and then nodded.

'Riders!'

'Yep! I figure that there are about four or five of the varmints!' Kid Palomino hastily dismounted. His gloved left hand held on tightly to the long leather reins as he stepped carefully closer to the edge of the high ridge.

'Too many trees to make out who they are.' Red rubbed his beard and slowly eased his mount forward.

'One thing's for certain, Red,' Palomino said. 'It

ain't the men that have been trailing us. That ain't Johnny Reno and his boys.'

'I got me a bad feeling about this, Kid!' Red admitted. 'I don't like this country. It ain't natural to have so many darn trees all over the place.'

'This sure ain't Texas and that's for sure, Red.' Palomino edged even closer to the crumbling ridge rim.

Suddenly the sound of firing filled both men's ears. The Kid could see distant plumes of smoke rising from below them amid the trees. Then the ground at his feet exploded as bullets drove into the hard soil. More shots followed and both men felt the heat of the lead as it passed within inches of them.

Kid Palomino darted back, grabbed his saddle horn and threw himself up on to the tall stallion. He hauled the reins hard to his right and drove his spurs into its flesh.

'Ride, Nugget! Ride! Get us out of here, boy!' the Kid screamed at his faithful steed.

Red Rivers slapped his long reins across the shoulders of his horse and galloped after his friend. The dust rose as the pair of riders headed down into the heart of a thicket of tall trees.

The Kid reined in his horse again. The palomino stallion drove its hoofs into the hard ground and halted.

'Who are they?' Red shouted as he stopped his buckskin mount.

'That's what I was trying to figure, *amigo*!' the Kid answered. He touched the top of his left shoulder and stared at the red droplets of blood that covered his gloved fingertips.

Red stood in his stirrups and reached across to his injured partner.

'You're wounded, Kid!' he exclaimed.

'Just a graze, Red,' Palomino responded as he vainly tried to see through the dense wall of trees in the direction of their attackers.

'We better head on out of here!'

Kid Palomino looked into the whiskered face.

'I ain't turning around and running from nobody!'

Red Rivers felt his heart sink. He knew that it was pointless trying to reason with his younger friend when he was in this frame of mind.

'OK! But we gotta try and get past them if'n we are ever going to reach Tent City!'

There was no emotion in the face of the handsome deputy as he stroked the cream-coloured neck of his horse.

'I don't cotton to folks using me for target practice, Red!'

'Me neither but we don't wanna get ourselves shot up before we reaches your pal Slim,' Red said. He could see the crimson blood soaking through his friend's denim jacket; he knew that the wound was worse than the Kid would admit to.

Kid Palomino nodded slowly. It was a reluctant admission that the older man was correct.

'I guess you're right, Red.'

Both horsemen hauled their reins to their left and

51

headed on through the trees.

They had travelled about a hundred yards when more shots lit up the shadows through which they were riding. The bark burst off the trees in front of them.

Palomino reached back, pulled his Winchester from its scabbard, then dropped off the back of his trusty horse. He slapped the rear of the tall animal and sent it thundering away from the scene as more bullets sent more tree-bark splintering all over him.

He cranked the mechanism of the rifle down and up again and watched his partner jump down into a ditch beside him.

'They want a fight, Red!' the Kid growled. 'I intend giving them one.'

Red watched as his own mount went racing after the palomino stallion.

'Darn that horse. He done took my carbine with him.'

Kid Palomino squinted into the darkness of the trees. He knew that the gunmen were there but could not see them. He tossed the rifle to his seated friend, then drew both his Colts from their holsters and cocked their hammers.

'Where are they?'

'Who are they?' Red added.

Another volley of shots came at them. This time the Kid saw the tell-tale signs of smoke a few hundred yards away from them.

'Whoever they are, they got enough cover to soak up all our ammunition, Red,' Palomino complained.

'I can't get a clear shot at them coz I can't see them.'

Red crawled to the side of the tall square-jawed man.

'That graze is bleeding bad, Kid. Your jacket is soaking up your blood like a sponge. You needs tending to, boy.'

Kid Palomino glanced down into the concerned face.

'Go get me a doctor!'

'I'm serious, Kid!'

The Kid nodded and then gritted his teeth.

'I know you are, old friend. I'm sorry. I just don't like the way this day is going.'

Red sighed. 'If'n we wait here, they gotta come to us. We can pick them off when they reach the clearing.'

Before the Kid could respond, they heard the sound of distant shots far beyond their own attackers. Whoever it was who had opened up on the two lawmen was now aiming their rifles at someone else.

'You hear that?' Kid Palomino leaned against the side of the tree he had chosen to use as a shield.

'You bet! Them riflemen seem to have found themselves another fight. One that don't involve us!' There was a mixture of anger and relief in the voice of the older deputy.

'You thinking what I'm thinking, Red?'

'I got me a feeling that Johnny Reno and his men have ridden into them varmints,' Red replied.

Kid Palomino nodded.

'If it *is* Johnny Reno who's been trailing us, I

reckon them riflemen will have a darn tough battle on their hands. He's one mean *hombre* according to his wanted posters.'

'At least they've stopped shootin' at us!' Red spat at the ground.

'Yep!' The Kid shrugged.

Red rose to his feet and gripped the sleeve of the brooding younger lawman.

'Let's get our horses and light on out of here, *amigo*! We got us an appointment in Tent City.'

Kid Palomino lowered the hammers of his Colts and then slid both pistols into their hand-tooled holsters. He turned away from the sound of the raging gun battle and followed Red down the slope in the direction that their mounts had taken.

'I hate to admit it, Red.'

'Admit what?'

'You're right again. Lets get out of this place.'

Johnny Reno had led four of his best men right into the jaws of the furious rifles. Without pausing even for a second, he had ordered his gang to dismount, fan out and return the fire they had ridden into.

The ruthless outlaw had known that there was trouble ahead of his gunmen for more than five minutes before they had reached the small clearing.

The sight that met their eyes, as they found the deadly rifles turned on them instead of Kid Palomino, chilled them to the bone.

Five Sioux warriors were seated astride their painted ponies firing after the fleeing deputies. The honed instincts of the Indians knew instantly that more white men had ridden along the narrow trail behind them.

Even the experienced Johnny Reno had never witnessed such horsemanship as the young braves displayed. The five Sioux swung their mounts around and instantly attacked the new intruders.

Steering their ponies with their legs, the warriors aimed, fired and then reloaded at full gallop.

There had been only seconds to spare for Reno and his followers to throw themselves from their mounts and find cover.

'What goes on here, Reno?' the outlaw called Luke screamed out as he felt a bullet tearing through his fleshy leg muscles.

Johnny Reno had no time to reply. He had drawn both his long-barrelled Remingtons and started to fire through the swirling dust that the unshod Indian ponies were kicking up as their masters circled their shocked targets.

Reno fired once, then again. His bony thumbs pulled the hammers of his guns back immediately the triggers had been squeezed.

His accurate bullets took one Sioux buck off his pony. His cruel eyes watched the limp brave crash into the hard ground.

Another of the warriors kicked his pony hard and forced the animal to jump over the heads of the firing outlaws. As he turned and fired his rifle, Reno fired two more deadly shots.

The three remaining Sioux drove their ponies

straight at the terrified gunmen. One called Smith went to move when he was hit by the bullets of two of the Indians rifles. Blood spewed all over the remaining outlaws as Smith fell backwards lifelessly.

Johnny Reno stood and fired again and again.

His lethal aim brought down all three ponies a mere six feet in front of him. The Sioux braves cascaded over the ground and crashed into Reno and Luke.

The wounded outlaw cried out in agony as the young warrior closest to him drew his knife and drove it into him.

Johnny Reno cocked his hammers again and fired straight into the heads of the two Indians beside him. Leaping to his feet he saw the crazed Sioux buck charging straight at him.

He pulled at the triggers of both his weapons but knew that his shots had not managed to stop the ferocious attacker. The outlaw leader could see the blood dripping from the knife-blade as the Indian kept coming.

Then the sound of a scattergun being fired deafened Reno.

Before he could step aside and cock his pistols again, he watched the young Indian being torn apart by the sheer power of the blast.

What was left of the Indian fell at Reno's feet.

His cold eyes darted all about him until he was convinced that every one of the Indians had been dispatched to the happy hunting grounds.

Joe Walker rose to his feet with the scattergun in

his hands. Smoke wisped from its twin barrels as the outlaw stepped over the bodies and approached Reno.

'I reckon you owe me a drink, Reno,' Walker drawled. He shook the spent cartridges from the smoking shotgun and then slid two new ones into the waiting chambers.

'I owe you a bottle, Joe,' Reno replied drily. 'I was a goner if you hadn't have killed him.'

'What made these Indians so ornery?' The last of Reno's men, named Davis, asked as he got to his feet and surveyed the carnage all around them. 'I thought that these Sioux were friendly to whites.'

'I reckon that they don't like the fact that a certain George Custer has brought a lot of gold-miners into their land, Davis,' Reno answered. 'Can't say I blame these poor critters for getting a tad angry.'

'Who in tarnation is George Custer?'

'A soldier boy who killed a lot of folks in the war,' Reno replied. 'The Indians call him Yellow Hair.'

'Luke's dead,' Walker said coldly.

'So is Smith.' Davis added.

'So there are just three of us left.' Reno holstered his guns and looked at the two men before him. 'I figure that'll be enough though.'

SEVEN

Slim Harper checked his pocket-watch for the tenth time in as many minutes. It was nearly noon. Since his encounter with Hooper Blake he had walked over every square inch of Tent City trying to buy a buckboard or wagon. It had been a vain quest. For some reason, no one appeared either willing or able to help him.

It seemed as if he was doomed to remain within the confines of the sea of tents at the mercy of Hooper Blake and his henchmen.

But men like Slim Harper never quit. He would keep trying to find what he sought as long as he had breath in his body. There was no way that he would give up. For Slim knew that Blake had his eye on him and would strike like a venomous viper at the first opportunity.

Slim closed the silver lid of his watch and returned it to his vest pocket. He stared up and down the busy street and tried to think of someone who might be willing to sell him transport out of this place.

There had to be someone in Tent City who was either brave enough or stupid enough to defy Hooper Blake and his deadly gunfighters.

But who and where was he?

The lean figure turned and began walking down the long straight thoroughfare toward the telegraph office. It seemed an eternity since he had sent his wire to Kid Palomino asking for help. The Kid had wired back saying that he was on his way with Red Rivers, but that now seemed such a long time ago.

Slim glanced up the side street at the huge wooden building with the word SALOON painted on its façade. He had not touched a drop of liquor since first arriving in Tent City, but was surely tempted now. Yet however much he craved to escape from the worry that now filled his every thought, he knew that he had to remain sober.

To survive, Slim needed every one of his wits about him.

He entered the tent and looked straight at the portly figure seated behind the desk next to the telegraph apparatus.

'Have I had any messages from Kid Palomino, John?'

'Not since the last one, Slim,' the man responded.

'Thanks!' Slim rubbed his chin and nodded at the man. He wondered how long it took to travel the distance between Waco and this unholy place.

When would the Kid arrive?

The question kept gnawing into the brain of the troubled man.

He stared back along the street. The sun was drying the mud at last but he did not notice. Slim began retracing his steps to the Angel Hotel. With every stride of his long thin legs, he thought about the eyes of Hooper Blake.

They had almost burned their way into his soul.

The gold-miner knew that he had been given a warning and it was up to him to heed it. Rumours of the fate of those who had ignored the gunfighter were rife in Tent City. Slim had no intention of joining them in their unmarked graves dotted out along the foothills.

A noise caught the attention of the lean man.

Slim paused and watched as a crowd of laughing men carried roosters across the street before him. There was going to be a cockfight tournament this afternoon, he recalled. His eyes narrowed and focused on the razor-sharp spurs that had been tied to the legs of the already angry birds. Those roosters would fight to the death and his fellow gold-miners would lap up every second of it.

These men would wager a small fortune on the winning birds of the bloody spectacles.

But Slim had no stomach for that sort of entertainment. All he wanted to do was get out of Tent City with his gold and return to his long-suffering wife and daughter. It was a feat that he was beginning to realize he might not be able to achieve.

'You're lookin' for a wagon, I'm told.'

The voice was familiar. Slim turned and stared into the face of Fred Smith, the owner of the hotel. He had never seen the man so obviously drunk before.

'Yep. I'm looking for something strong enough to carry the weight of my three wooden chests, Fred,' Slim replied.

Smith began to sway. The smell of stale whiskey cut through the distance between the two men.

'I got me a wagon and team you can buy, Harper.'

Slim nodded. 'How much is this gonna cost me, Fred?'

'Two sacks of gold nuggets,' the hotel owner mumbled. 'I figure that it's cheap considering you can't seem to get nobody else to do business with you.'

Slim Harper turned and continued walking in the direction of the Angel. The drunken hotel man tried to keep up with the younger fitter man.

'Two sacks? Are you serious?'

'I figure that it's a bargain. I heard Hooper Blake talkin' with his boys an hour back.' Fred Smith's words managed to stop Slim in his tracks. 'It wasn't good.'

'What does that mean, Fred?' Slim looked at the red cheeks on the plump face before him. 'What are you trying to tell me?'

Smith moved up to the taller man and leaned against the thin figure.

'He's planning to kill you, boy!'

'I already figured that out, Fred.' Slim sighed. 'Why else do you think I'm so set on leaving Tent City? If I stay here he's gonna get even angrier with me. I have to try and get out of this damn town even if it is darn risky.'

Smith waved a finger under Slim's nose.

'You don't understand. He and his boys were planning how to get rid of you tonight after sundown. They intend making you disappear permanent. Real permanent.'

The words chilled Slim Harper to the marrow. He took the elbow of the drunken Fred Smith and led him away from the hotel and in the direction of the large wooden saloon.

'Where we goin', Harper?' Smith enquired as he felt himself being carried along in his companion's strong grip.

'To the saloon, Fred,' Slim replied.

'But I just come from there.'

'I'm kinda thirsty, Fred. You'll share a bottle with me, won't you?' Slim guided the hotelier straight at the large building.

By the time Smith had managed to open his mouth again, the two men had pushed their way into the dark interior of the saloon.

'Oh, we're here already!' Smith said looking around the almost empty bar. 'I reckon I could manage a few more shots of whiskey.'

Slim dragged the the staggering man by the elbow to the long bar and aimed a finger at the bartender.

'A bottle of rye.'

The bartender accepted the silver coins from Slim, then placed a black glass bottle before them.

Slim picked up the bottle and two thimble glasses from a crystal pyramid of stacked tumblers and then led Smith to a nearby table.

'Kinda quiet in here, ain't it?' he noted.

'The cockfights,' Smith muttered, staring at the bottle between them on the damp surface of the round table. 'Everyone has gone to the cockfights. I prefer my chicken fried.'

Slim pulled the cork from the neck of the bottle and inhaled the aroma of the crude liquor. He wondered how many days it had been since the spirit had been distilled and bottled.

'Do you agree the price? Two bags of gold seems kinda reasonable to me.' Smith grinned across the table at the younger man. A man he knew was at his mercy.

'Two bags of gold, you say?' Slim repeated the amount as he poured the amber liquor into the pair of glasses.

Fred Smith lifted his glass and downed the drink in one swallow. He had drunk so much whiskey in the previous hour that his throat was immune to the burning liquid.

'Yeah. Two bags. You got more than enough gold in them chests. You'd not miss two bags. Not when it will enable you to get out of this damn town.'

Slim thought about it for a few moments and then nodded at the man he had never quite trusted.

'You're right, Fred. Two bags is a reasonable price for a wagon and team.'

Fred Smith lifted the bottle, poured himself another measure and downed it quickly. Then he repeated the action.

'I reckon that it's probably the only chance you've

got to survive the night, Harper.'

'I thought that Blake didn't want to make a move on me while I'm holed up in town. How come he changed his mind?' Slim was staring straight at the older man trying to work out if he was lying or not. It was a hard call to make.

Fred downed his whiskey and grinned broadly.

'He's greedy, boy. He also ain't blessed with a lot of patience. He figures that if he and his boys rough you up tonight, they can take you out of Tent City and dispose of your body in the foothills. Then them three chests of gold are his.'

Slim picked up his own glass and sipped at the liquor.

'How do you know all this? Since when does Hooper Blake talk about his killing plans in front of anyone?'

Smith filled his glass once again.

'I was in the next room to his. Remember, the walls are only made of canvas. I heard every word. The whole thing. That's why I decided to come out and get myself drunk.'

'You succeeded.' Slim smiled thoughtfully.

'I can have my wagon hitched up and moved to the rear of the hotel just after dark. All you gotta do is put them chests on the flatbed and then head on out.' Smith took another drink. 'I'll tell Hooper and his boys that you went to have a word with the soldier boys. He'll not go anywhere near them varmints. By the time he figures out that you've left Tent City, you ought to have enough distance between you to reach civilization before they can catch up with you.'

Slim toyed with his glass.

'I'm trying to figure out exactly why you would want to help me, Fred.'

'I don't. I want them two bags of gold nuggets,' Smith retorted. 'Then whatever happens between you and Blake won't trouble me coz I'll still have me those little yellow stones.'

'Brutally honest.'

'It's just business, Harper. Just business.'

'What if Blake finds out that you helped me?'

'He won't,' Smith said firmly. 'All I want is some of that gold and if neither of us tells Hooper about it, he'll never know.'

Slim Harper agreed with every single word that came from the lips of the hotel owner. The trouble was, the man no longer sounded as drunk as he had only a few minutes earlier.

'You sure have it all worked out, Fred. I'll give you that.'

Smith raised his glass and smiled.

'I'm a businessman, boy. That's what I do. I figure things out so there's a profit in it.'

'Some folks would say that kinda thinking is a little cold-blooded.' Slim frowned.

'So what?'

Slim finished his rye and placed the thimble glass down on to the table. As the whiskey burned its way down toward his belly, the gold-miner nodded to the seated hotel owner.

'I hate to admit it but we've got ourselves a deal,

Fred,' Slim said reluctantly.

'Good. You won't regret this.'

Slim Harper rose slowly to his full height and touched the brim of his hat.

'I'll head on back to the hotel, Fred. I'll get those two bags of gold ready for you when you return. We can sort out the details later.'

'I'll just finish off this mighty fine bottle of whiskey, Harper,' Fred Smith said, lifting the bottle and shaking its contents. 'I hate waste.'

'OK! I'll expect you in about an hour.'

Slim turned and moved towards the swing doors and the glaring sunlight that bathed the sea of canvas. He made his way out into the street until the haunting sounds of the nearby cockfight filled his ears.

For the first time since he had been confronted by the intimidating Hooper Blake, Slim felt that he just might have a chance of escaping Tent City for good.

Fred Smith chuckled as he watched the thin figure walking in the direction of his hotel. He stared out through the window and poured himself yet another measure of the fiery liquid.

Then the sound of footsteps came out from the shadows behind the seated hotelier. Fred Smith turned his head and looked up into the grinning face of Hooper Blake.

'You hear all that, Hoop?' Smith asked.

'Every word, Fred,' Blake replied, patting the man on the shoulder. 'You did good. Real good.'

EIGHT

The two deputies had followed the small stream down from the very top of the forested hill until the ground levelled out. They could see the crystal-clear water heading straight into the heart of the sea of canvas tents about ten miles ahead. The magnificent palomino stallion had obeyed every one of its master's commands over the previous four hours. It had been a long hard ride down through the trees, a journey that had only been halted for the animal to be watered and to allow the smaller buckskin quarter horse to catch up.

A cool chill was now enveloping them as the stars began to force their way out into the vast heavens above them. At last the sun was submitting and reluctantly sinking out of the big sky and allowing the night to rule this dangerous land.

Neither of the horsemen had tried to find out who it was shooting it out on the high ridge far behind them. All they had been concerned about was that the rifles had ceased firing their deadly bullets at them.

They had taken advantage of their attackers' confusion and ridden as fast as their mounts could carry them down through the trees until they could no longer hear the battle being waged behind them in the high mountainous landscape.

Kid Palomino pulled back on his reins and stopped his tired mount.

'Easy, Nugget.'

Red Rivers' quarter horse pulled up next to him and the older man leaned over his saddle horn. Every sinew in his body hurt.

'How's your shoulder, Palomino?' Red asked.

'I figure it's stopped bleeding,' the Kid replied. 'It don't hurt none any more.'

The terrain before them was flat and covered in a sea of tents. The sky was crimson with a million stars growing brighter as the sun slipped down behind the distant hills. Both riders dismounted and rested on the hard ground.

'Is that it?' Red asked rubbing the sweat and grime off his face with the tails of his bandanna. 'Is that Tent City?'

Kid Palomino exhaled and tilted his head until he was looking straight at his friend.

'Reckon so, Red.'

'I guess they got the name right anyway.' Red tried to loosen up his stiff joints after the painfully long ride. Every movement of his arms seemed to make a loud clicking sound.

'You figure that maybe you're getting a little old for this life, partner?' Palomino winked.

Red scratched his whiskers. 'I might require oilin' a little but I'm still twice the man you are.'

'Twice as old anyway,' the Kid added.

Red stared down at the strange settlement. He had never seen so many tents in one place before.

'It's still a ways off, Kid. A least a couple of hours' ride.'

'And it's nearly dark,' the Kid noted, looking up at the sky above them. 'I reckon we ought to feed the horses and have us some grub before we head on in to Tent City. The trouble is, I hate being so close and not finishing our journey, *amigo*.'

Red nodded in agreement.

'Yeah. I know what you mean.'

Palomino pushed his gloved hands on to the hard ground and managed to force himself back up on to his feet. He was tired and it showed.

'I'll water the horses. You make a camp-fire, Red. I want some coffee before we carry on.'

Red scrambled to his feet, moved to his saddle-bags and undid the buckle on the closest satchel.

'You figure that Johnny Reno and his cronies are still doggin' our trail?'

The Kid removed his Stetson and dropped it before the hoofs of his lathered-up palomino stallion. He glanced up at the tall trees, which were now mostly behind them. He shrugged.

'I ain't too sure, Red. I've not had the feeling that we've been followed ever since those riflemen opened up on us. But I could be wrong. Reno ain't the sort to quit so easy, though. Not if he thinks that there's a few bucks to be made.'

'But what would make him think that there might be money to be made by trailin' us?' Red asked.

'Coz we ignored the price on his head and lit out,' the Kid replied. 'Reno must reckon that we know of something that's worth more than the bounty his wanted poster carries. Reno ain't dumb. He'd trail us into the bowels of Hell if'n he thought that he might make a few bucks.'

Red nodded as he pulled the small black coffee pot out of the satchel, then he sighed wearily.

'The hairs on my neck ain't stopped tingling since we caught back up with our horses and rode out of that turkey shoot. I reckon that someone is still following us. I ain't seen them, but they're up there in the trees OK. I can almost smell the critters. It has to be Reno.'

'Yep. Only Johnny Reno would be so hard to shake off.'

'There ain't no sign of him now though, Kid.'

'Maybe they lost our trail.' Palomino picked one of his canteens off the saddle horn and slowly unscrewed its stopper. He continued looking up at the trees as if knowing that his partner was right. 'Lets eat and have us some coffee, Red. I ain't never been so tuckered out as I am right now. I need something in my belly that'll keep my eyes open when we reach Tent City.'

Red tossed his own hat to his pal and began to gather up kindling as he watched Palomino pouring water into both hats for their horses to drink out of.

The wily older deputy knew that they and their exhausted mounts needed rest. Red said nothing as he prepared the black beverage by adding coffee grounds to the last of their water in the pot.

He knew that Kid Palomino had no equals with his matched pair of Colts, but the youthful deputy could and often did make mistakes.

The Kid had always been guided by his desire to help those less able than himself. He had risked his life countless times since the two men had first met. It was a quality which also had a darker side though.

The Kid would often let his heart rule his head. It was a dangerous way to live, even if it did prove successful for the most part. Red had lost count of how many times he had followed Palomino, against his own better judgement, into a raging gunfight.

Kid Palomino would always leap before he looked.

Yet there was something different in the way the Kid was acting since he had received the telegraph message from the man called Slim. In all the years they had ridden together, Red had never heard his partner even mention anyone named Slim before and yet he had dropped everything in Waco to answer the plea for help.

Why?

Thoughtfully, Red continued to prepare the coffee and found the last of their beef jerky. He knew that he had to try and get his partner ready for what might lie in wait for them in the distant Tent City. If history was anything to go by, the Kid was riding straight into trouble.

The bearded man knew that to get Palomino to rest was almost impossible, but if the younger lawman thought that their horses were exhausted, he might at least be willing to spend an hour drinking coffee before they continued on the final leg of their journey.

Kid Palomino looked at the settlement before them as blazing torches and oil-lamps were lit in a vain attempt to fend off the coming of night. He pulled the gloves off his hands and tucked them into his gunbelt as the two horses finished drinking from their upturned hats.

'You know that we could get to Tent City before that coffee brews, Red,' the Kid noted in a frustrated tone.

'Sit down and rest up, Kid,' Red suggested as he placed more and more kindling on to the small fire beneath the coffee pot.

Reluctantly, the younger lawman obeyed.

'I keep wondering if Slim is OK. We've taken a darn long time getting here. He might be dead already.'

'We've pushed our horses a lot harder than most men would have done, Palomino,' Red Rivers said. He touched the side of the black pot to check how hot its contents were. 'My old Derby is about ready to drop and Nugget ain't gonna carry you for much longer before he pulls up lame or makes a mistake and puts a leg in a gopher hole.'

The Kid knew his friend was right. He rose to his feet, moved to the two horses and undid their cinch straps. Then he hauled the heavy Texan saddles from their backs and dropped them on the ground.

He pulled out a bag of grain from his saddle-bags, poured its contents in front of the two animals and stood watching as they ate.

'I ain't never seen you so jittery before, Palomino.'

'It might be coz I got myself winged back there.' The Kid sat down again next to his friend and warmed his hands in the flames of the fire.

'You've been jittery since you got that wire in Waco,' Red said, as he unfolded the wrapping on the beef jerky and pulled a small knife from his vest pocket. 'I ain't never seen you like this. How come?'

Palomino ignored the question. 'I reckon you're right, Red. Another hour or so ain't gonna make a lot of difference.'

Red Rivers cut a slice of jerky off the small slab and handed it to his pal.

'Eat!'

The Kid began to eat.

NINE

Tent City was an even wilder place after the sun set. The sound of guns being fired into the air as men celebrated the results of the day's labour was a constant reminder that this was no ordinary settlement. For this was where every one of the prospecting gold-miners returned after tearing the precious gold nuggets and dust from their claims.

The noise which grew louder and louder as darkness returned to Tent City was ignored by all its inhabitants. All except Slim Harper. For he knew that his time was running out like the sand in an hourglass. Every bullet that was fired into the heavens felt like a new nail in his coffin.

He knew that this night was no different from all the scores that had preceded it. Men with their valuable discoveries burning holes in their pockets wanted to buy themselves another night's pleasure. They knew nothing of the fate which Slim had been told awaited him.

As always, the darkness of night brought Tent City

back to life. The hundreds of miners who flooded back were greeted by the men and women who would spend the entire night trying to part them from their hard-earned ore.

Yet none of this meant a thing to Slim Harper.

All the gold-miner knew was that he had been living on borrowed time since his meeting at breakfast with the brutal Hooper Blake and his hired gunmen.

But it had not been the words that had spewed from the mouth of Blake himself that had troubled Slim for the remainder of the day. It had been the ones which Fred Smith had gushed out over countless drinks of whiskey at noon in the saloon.

Those words had chilled him to the bone.

For the first time since he had sold his claim and taken shelter in the Angel Hotel, Slim knew that Hooper Blake had his sights on him and his treasure.

It was not a comforting thought.

It now looked as if Kid Palomino would not arrive in time to help escort him safely out of Tent City. Maybe the young deputy had fallen prey to someone out on the hazardous trail? It was a thought that kept returning to the fevered brain of the troubled miner.

Slim knew that he now had to act alone if he were to have a chance of surviving. He could no longer wait for Kid Palomino to arrive in Tent City.

There simply was no more time.

For all he knew the displaced Sioux warriors might have attacked the Kid and his friend Red Rivers when they rode into the land known simply as the Black

Hills. Even Kid Palomino could not fight off a band of angry Indians.

Slim took another mouthful of water from the jug next to his crude cot.

Fred Smith had made it very clear that he had overheard Blake talking with his ruthless men planning his disappearance and murder. The hotel owner had made it crystal clear that Blake wanted Slim's gold.

The room was now dark. Only stray light seemed to find its way through small breaks in the canvas walls where it was sewn together against the wooden framework. Slim knew that he could not risk lighting the oil-lamp that stood on the small dresser next to him. He had to give the impression that the room was empty.

Sweat ran from every pore in his body. Slim had remained in his room all through the long hot afternoon, waiting for Fred Smith to return from the saloon. The four canvas walls had made the room like a Turkish bath. He was soaked in his own sweat yet knew that it was probably far safer to remain there than out on the streets where Blake and his men could watch his every move.

Now, as miners fired their guns into the sky, Slim knew that Blake's men could easily pick him off with a well-placed 'stray' bullet.

Where was Smith?

Had the hotel owner fallen into a drunken stupor after finishing the bottle of rye? Another question that Slim knew would not be answered.

The gold-miner had waited all afternoon for Smith to return from the saloon and discuss their deal. Yet Smith had not come back at all.

Every passing minute had caused him to become more and more aware of his own shortcomings. He was no fighter. He had never been a fighter.

Slim had stayed silently in his room. He was afraid to make even the slightest of noises. For any sound could bring the gang crashing in on him with their knives and guns ready and able to snuff out his life for good.

What sort of man was he? It was a thought that had grown like a cancer in his mind as minutes turned into hours. What sort of man had to send for help? Why did he always need the help of men whom he secretly loathed?

He toyed with the brand new handgun that he had purchased ten days earlier, as if waiting for Hooper Blake to come crashing his way through the canvas wall at any moment.

Yet Slim knew nothing of guns. He had seen it loaded by the man in the hardware store, but had no idea of how to release its cylinder chamber himself. It was a heavy lump of metal that terrified him.

Slim held the gun at arm's length and wondered if he could use the deadly weapon if required to do so, without blowing his own foot off.

For Slim Harper had never been one of those men who lived their lives by their gun skills. He was simply someone who had spent his entire adult life chasing the elusive pot of gold at the end of the rainbow.

A man who had somehow managed to find his own pot of gold at long last. It had taken a wasted lifetime to achieve, but he could at last turn to face those who had doubted his dream.

All he had to do was survive!

The problem was, surviving Hooper Blake and his gunmen was a lot easier to say than do.

Slim knew that he had wasted his life in the pursuit of the golden nuggets that now filled his three wooden chests. He had married and fathered one child before finding it impossible to resist the overwhelming urge to start searching for his own personal bonanza.

The stories of men who had become wealthy by discovering a fortune in gold had haunted Slim Harper since his childhood. They had ruled his every waking moment. They had become his master and he was helpless to do anything but obey their siren call.

There had been so many years of travelling from one gold-strike to another. He hardly knew his wife any longer and would probably not even recognize his own daughter should their paths ever cross.

Only the faded old photograph that he carried at all times allowed him to recall their faces. But that was a memory captured in time and bore little relation to what they now looked like.

Like himself, they had grown older and the images were now nothing more than a faded reminder of what he had left behind him back in Cooper's City all those years before.

But all that would change now.

Of that, he was confident. Slim had gold.

Enough gold to make him rich.

Being rich would make him respectable. Slim knew that it could also make Edith and Sophie forgive him. At least he prayed that it would.

Eventually the lean man rose to his feet and stared at the three chests. Did they have the power to alter all the wrongs that he had done over the years?

Did the gold nuggets have that power?

How many men had asked themselves the same question?

Then beyond the locked, solid wooden door, Slim Harper heard footsteps and raised his gun in the direction of the sound which came drifting through the canvas walls all around him. His hand shook as he tried to keep the barrel aimed at the canvas walls.

He swallowed hard.

Was this Hooper Blake coming to lure him to his death?

A thousand thoughts raced through his brain. He continued listening to the approaching footsteps.

They grew closer and closer.

He somehow managed to pull the hammer of the Colt back until it locked fully into position.

Then he heard another set of footsteps coming from the opposite direction. Slim's eyes darted back and forth as he tried to work out where the two men were outside the canvas walls. Then both men stopped walking.

The door handle was turned but the lock held. He knew that they could slice their way through the canvas walls with a sharp knife to gain entry, but Blake and his followers were lazy. They would wait until they had a key.

His key!

Slim inhaled silently and strained to hear the low voices.

'Where is he?' Weaver asked.

'Smith said that he'd gone to the cavalry section to have a word with one of the officers,' Hooper Blake replied. 'I reckon he's scared. Darn scared. We'll take all the boys up to the saloon and cover every street between here and the army outpost. When he comes back, we'll grab the critter. Smash his brains out and then take him out to the foothills.'

'OK!'

Slim froze to the spot and had to stop his gun hand from shaking by grabbing his wrist with his left hand.

'C'mon, Weaver!' Blake growled.

'Right, Hoop.'

Slim heard both men walking off in the same direction. He suddenly heaved a huge sigh of relief as he recalled that Smith had told him that he would send the gunfighters off in the wrong direction.

Had Fred Smith actually told him the truth? It seemed so.

Then he heard more footsteps. This time he realized that they were shuffling steps. The sort Fred Smith made when he was real drunk.

'You in there, Harper?'

Slim grabbed at the door and unlocked it. It seemed strange to the gold-miner that a hotel made of canvas would still have wooden doors held in wooden frames, but he was thankful of even that small protection.

'Where in tarnation have you been, Fred?' Slim asked as he grabbed the man's sleeve and hauled him inside the small room. 'I've been melting in here all afternoon waiting for you to show up. What took you so long?'

Fred Smith rubbed his mouth along the back of his shirt sleeve.

'I tried to get here but Blake and his men have been all over this place for hours. He's had men out front and out back all afternoon. One in the saloon and another down by the hardware store. They've been looking out for you. Reckon they've got the scent of all your gold in their nostrils, boy.'

'What's happening now?'

'The plan is going well, Harper,' Smith said. 'I have my wagon being brought around back as we speak. I had to wait for the right time to tell Blake that I'd spoken with you and that you'd told me that you were going to see the soldier boys.'

Slim nodded.

'I heard them talking about that.'

'They've all headed up the street. They'll wait there all night for the chance of getting the drop on you.'

Slim grabbed two bags of gold off the bed and

handed them to the man. He recognized the smile that he had seen so many times on the faces of those who looked at the precious golden nuggets.

'Ready?' Smith asked.

Slim nodded.

TEN

There was a storm brewing. A real bad storm. Not just up in the sky above the two deputies' heads, but far off on the range that faced them. Lightning was already forking its way down from the angry black clouds far off to the south. The wind was gaining pace all about them as it signalled the coming of the awesome tempest.

Both lawmen knew that they had to continue on towards the strange mining community ahead of them. There was no shelter here and they knew how dangerous it was to be caught out in the open when a range storm hit.

It could destroy anything in its path like a crazed invisible monster.

'I don't like the look of that, Red.' Palomino pointed as he lowered the tin mug from his mouth. 'We'd better hightail it out of here darn fast.'

Red Rivers had already started to resaddle their mounts when he had first spotted the white flashes of lightning far to the south. The rumbling of thunder was growing louder with every passing moment.

'Darn right.' Kid Palomino poured the remnants of his coffee over what was left of the camp-fire and then used the side of his left boot to kick dust across the ashes. 'That storm's headed our way, Red.'

The older man tightened the last cinch strap of his horse, unhooked the stirrup off the saddle horn and dropped the fender. He moved to the nervous palomino stallion and lifted his partner's saddle off the ground. He threw it over top of the high blanket until it rested on the animal's shoulders. He carefully adjusted it until he was satisfied it was sitting squarely on the huge stallion.

'Yep. Reckon we have to try and get out of here before that lightning catches us out in the open.'

The Kid patted his pal on the back and finished saddling his horse as Red scooped up their bags off the ground, then strapped them on behind the high Texan cantles.

'Reckon we can outrun it?'

'I figure that storm's gonna swoop over the whole valley in the next couple of hours, Kid. There ain't gonna be no refuge anywhere.'

The Kid nodded in agreement.

'You're right. I just want to try and get these horses under some kinda cover before that lightning catches up with us.'

'Have we got enough time to get to Tent City before it does, Palomino?' Red looped his reins over the head of his quarter horse.

Kid Palomino stared at the distant storm. It was

moving fast like a black giant. The sky was lighting up as the flashes traced their way through the black swirling clouds. He had no answer for his friend.

'We can sure try and outride it, Red.'

'Yeah. The horses are rested up. They ought to be able to race a little storm.'

Palomino scooped his reins up. 'C'mon, Red. Reckon it's time we went and found Slim.'

Both men grabbed their saddle horns and hoisted themselves atop their horses. They gathered in their reins and turned their mounts until they were facing Tent City. They then spurred hard and gave their defiant Texan whooping call.

The two horsemen galloped toward the sea of tents. They were ready for anything either man or the elements could throw at them.

Fred Smith led the way out through maze of canvas corridors. He was followed by Slim Harper and two burly men. They each shared the burden of carrying the three heavy wooden chests that were filled with the precious golden ore. Smith led them out of the hotel and into the dark alley which backed on to the large temporary structure.

The men heaved the heavy chests up on to the flat bed of the wagon and then accepted money from the hotelier. They disappeared into the dark shadows within seconds of being paid.

Fred Smith moved closer to Slim and watched as he climbed up on to the back of the wagon and began dragging the wooden chests up toward the driver's seat. A large roll of tarpaulin was piled up right behind the long seat. Slim pulled at the end of the heavy fabric and covered the three chests. He then walked back along the vehicle and dropped down on to the hard ground.

Smith followed the taller man past the wheels. Slim made his way to the pair of matched black horses and carefully checked their harnesses until satisfied that everything was hitched up correctly.

'Does everything meet with your approval?' Smith asked the brooding man.

Slim had a bad feeling in his guts. He could not pinpoint what was making him so anxious, but he knew that something just did not feel right about all this.

'Seems OK, Fred,' Slim said at last.

The hotel owner smiled again.

'Now it's up to you, boy. You have to get as far away from Tent City as you can. Put distance between you and Hooper Blake.'

Slim nodded.

'Yeah. Reckon there's enough night to allow me to get a good way out of this land.'

The clouds above them were fast-moving and angry. The stars could no longer be seen as the wind increased its pace across the heavens.

Slim pulled at the front of his jacket until he was able to do up the large buttons. He watched Smith scurrying back into the back door of his hotel. It was like watching a rodent moving from one pile of filth to another.

He shuddered and turned his collar up until it covered his neck. He wondered if it was the cold or something else that had made him shiver.

Slim hauled himself up the side of the tall wagon and sat down on the driver's seat. Even now he wondered if he might just run into Kid Palomino.

Unwrapping the long leather reins from around the brake-pole, Slim inhaled deeply and then released the brake. He slapped the reins on to the backs of the team and allowed the wagon to make its way slowly along the uneven ground between the tents.

There was no going back now, he thought. This time Slim had to keep going. He had to try and put distance between himself and those who wanted not only his gold, but his life as well.

The wagon snaked its way into the blackness and out of the settlement.

Hooper Blake walked down the side of the hotel with Franks and Weaver at his side. He struck a match with his thumbnail and cupped the flame to the end of his long cigar. Smoke drifted from his teeth as he stared at the wagon disappearing into the shadows.

His cold ruthless eyes moved to his left when he heard the rear door of the hotel opening. He watched Fred Smith walking cautiously toward him. The hotel owner was grinning broadly.

'Well?'

'You did good, Fred,' Hooper Blake responded. 'Harper didn't suspect a damn thing, did he?'

Smith beamed.

'Nope. He thinks he's safe. That dumb fool believed everything I told him.'

Blake looked up at the quickly altering sky. There was no sign of concern in his stone-hard features. He had a plan and was convinced nothing could prevent him from reaping the bounty of the destructive seeds he had already sown.

'Good.' Blake waved a hand at his two gunfighters. 'Go get the horses, boys.'

Fred Smith stepped closer to Blake as Weaver and Franks obeyed their boss's orders and ran off to get their mounts.

'Where's Bronson, Hoop?' Smith asked curiously.

Hooper Blake smiled before putting the cigar between his teeth.

'He's in the wagon under the tarp, Fred.'

ELEVEN

There was a desperation in the hands of Slim Harper as he brought the heavy leather reins down on to the backs of the matched pair of black horses between the wagon traces. They responded once again. The team quickened their pace and reluctantly drove on toward the gathering storm.

To the gold-miner it seemed as if he were heading straight into the jaws of Hell itself.

But Slim could not allow himself the luxury of fearing what was ahead when he knew exactly the deadly dangers behind him were far worse.

He whipped the reins over the heads of the team again and again urging them to find greater and greater speed. The wide-eyed team dutifully obeyed their new master. Their hoofs tore up the hard unyielding ground in their vain attempt to get away from the driver cracking the reins behind them.

For the first time since he had taken refuge in the Angel Hotel, Slim felt as if he might just have a chance of fleeing the guns of Hooper Blake and his hired killers. All he had to do was keep the team moving for the entire night and he would be too far away from the deadly gunmen for them ever to catch up with him.

Slim knew that there was no time to lose. Every second was as precious as the gold ore in the three wooden chests behind him on the flatbed under the tarp.

The clock was ticking.

Would he manage to reach safety before Blake realized that he had been tricked? The question kept screaming inside his mind.

All he had to do was reach the distant pass and the Black Hills would be nothing but a memory. Then he would be free to head on to Texas and Cooper's City and find Edith and Sophie.

It seemed so simple and yet Slim realized that the odds were stacked against him. For once Blake figured out that he had been duped he would mount up and start following.

And saddle horses could gallop far faster than the two harnessed between the traces. Saddle horses were not laden down hauling a heavy wagon. Slim glanced over his shoulder at the darkness behind him. He could still see the lanterns and torches of Tent City behind him.

He was still far too close to the settlement.

Lightning splintered out of the brooding black sky and cut its way through the cold air ahead of him. The haunting white light blinded Slim for a second as it lit up the range all around him.

Slim gritted his teeth and continued to force the

terrified team on towards the raging storm.

Rain started to fall across the barren range with more and more ferocity. It felt like the stings of a million crazed hornets hitting his face, but the gold-miner kept whipping the two horses to gain even more speed.

The sound of rumbling thunder clouds was mixed with a strange howling noise. Slim had never heard anything like it in his entire life. It sounded as if a thousand wolves were howling at the moonless sky.

It was as if the storm was alive!

Waiting to devour him.

A creature warning that it could and would destroy anything bold enough to challenge its authority.

Slim's eyes darted heavenward as even more burn-ing white flashes of electricity streaked through the black swirling clouds. He could barely believe the speed of the lightning as it moved unchecked above him.

It was a power that no mere mortal could under-stand or possibly comprehend. It was not subject to the same rules that men like Slim Harper had to obey.

It took every ounce of his strength to control the team of black horses. He could feel the muscles in his powerful arms almost bursting through his shirt and jacket sleeves as he held on to the flesh ripping reins.

Every time the white lightning flashed, Slim could see blood on his hands where the reins had almost been torn from his grip. It was only the fact that he had spent half his life swinging a pickaxe that enabled him to remain in control of the powerful horses.

But even torn flesh and bleeding hands could not stop him now. He would never quit. The stakes were far too high even to acknowledge defeat.

When Slim had left Tent City he had believed that he was headed into just another storm. He had seen hundreds of them in his years out in the wilderness. The true magnitude of the danger had taken longer to dawn on him.

Now he knew exactly what faced him.

This was something that only came along once in most men's lifetimes. Most men would never be faced with anything so utterly destructive. But Slim knew he had to keep the horses going. He just had to keep them going.

However much the horses tried to fight him, Slim continued forcing them into the mouth of the monster.

Lightning forked down all around the wagon as it thundered across the ground. Trees exploded and burst into flames as the powerful violence of the lethal electricity twisted down through the charged air and hit its earthly targets.

He pressed his left boot against the wooden boards at the front of the driver's box to steady himself and lashed the tails of the long reins down across the backs of the two charging horses again.

Slim glanced again over his shoulder. There was still no sign of Hooper Blake and his men. Then he began to realize that no sane man would ride out into this nightmare unless driven by something far more terrifying. Slim knew that the fear of being killed by Blake was far greater than facing the tempest before him. No amount of gold was worth risking your neck for.

Again the flat valley lit up.

Ahead of the fast-moving wagon, it was just possible to see where the tree-covered hills closed in on the flat range leaving only a narrow pass to negotiate the way out of the Black Hills.

Slim was confident that once he got through the pass, he would be out of danger.

He doubted if Hooper Blake and his men would ever venture that far away from the rich pickings of Tent City. Even to get his gold. There was plenty more back in the canvas settlement waiting to be taken from the other gold-miners.

All he had to do was reach and get through that pass. But it would be another a couple of hours before the wagon would even get close to that point.

The rain was now cutting into his face like razors as the wind grew more powerful. Slim screwed up his eyes and tried to see but it was only possible when the lightning exploded above him.

With every mile that the wagon managed to progress over the flat range, the less troubled he became. He knew the danger that was now engulfing him was totally unpredictable but he was unafraid.

Then the sheer power of the storm hit the horses head on. It was like crashing into a solid wall of invisible demons. The team of black horses had almost stopped as the sheer force of the wind and rain engulfed them. Slim pushed his right boot down on the brake-pole and then wrapped the reins around his broad muscular shoulders.

The ferocious anger of the storm now smashed brutally into the vehicle. A thousand bare-knuckled fists could not have inflicted more pain on the horses or their helpless master. All they could do was stand and take it.

And take it they did!

Slim felt his hat being torn off his head and the heavy wagon beneath him being rocked as if it were no heavier than a feather. He hung on to the reins and the wooden seat for all he was worth as rain lashed down.

Slim turned and looked down on to the flatbed of the wagon at his large tarpaulin. He could just make out the shapes of his three wooden chests beneath it. The wagon was shaking and being lifted off the ground but the gold-miner somehow managed to remain on the driver's seat.

Then Slim's eyes narrowed even more.

The tarpaulin was moving. But it was not the storm causing it to shift. It was something else.

Something beneath it!

A huge deafening eruption directly above him illuminated the entire range. The horses reared up in their traces and tried to bolt but Slim kept his right boot pressed firmly down on the long brake-pole.

For a split second, Slim's attention was drawn to

the two frightened horses. When he looked back at the flatbed he could see a man clambering out from beneath the soaked tarp. It was like watching a serpent slithering from its lair as the left hand emerged into the driving rain.

Slim was in total shock.

His mind raced as he tried to work out who it was that had been hiding under the tarpaulin since he had left Tent City. His blood froze in his veins as the sudden realization dawned on him.

Fred Smith had been working with Hooper Blake all the time!

They had to be in cahoots for Bronson to have been secreted on to the wagon!

Quickly, Slim pulled the heavy reins off his shoulder and wrapped them around the tall brake-pole. He tried to turn to face the intruder as the violent wind fought him every inch of the way.

Bronson's cold eyes sparkled in the flashing light as he tried to focus on his target. Then the gunslinger saw the bedraggled figure above him.

Slim tried to speak but his words were lost in the deafening noise that had overwhelmed them.

Then to his sheer horror, he saw the gleaming gun in Bronson's hand. He tried to find his own holstered weapon, but it was too late.

A flash of blinding light spewed from the barrel of Bronson's gun and tore through the distance between the two men.

Slim felt the bullet pass within inches of his face as he leapt down on to the kneeling figure. Another shot blasted from the gun in Bronson's hand.

The exhausted miner clenched his fist and punched the chin of the larger man. Both figures fell on to the soaked tarp. Another punch from Slim's fist caught the gunman's jaw. Bronson's back hit the concealed chests and he screamed out in agony. But the sound was drowned out in the howling of the storm which was moving over the wagon.

Bronson felt the strong grip of his foe holding the wrist of his gun hand. He reached up and clawed at Slim's eyes and forced him back.

Both men rose to their feet and wrestled as the wagon beneath them shook backwards and forth. Slim saw the barrel of the gun turn and aim at him.

The gun fired again. The bullet missed its target but the blinding hot powder sent Slim staggering backwards. He tried to find his attacker but it was impossible.

Bronson steadied himself and then cocked the hammer of his weapon again. This time he made no mistake.

The gun blasted again.

Slim Harper felt himself being lifted up into the air by the force of the bullet ripping into him. By the time Bronson had risen over the hidden chests, he had managed to fire his gun again and again until its chambers were empty.

What was left of Slim Harper landed between the two terried horses and rested limply on the wagon traces.

Bronson clambered over the driver's seat and

stared down at the body hanging across the wooden traces.

Slim Harper was quite dead.

TWELVE

Hooper Blake stared into the driving rain and continued laughing to himself. The cigar between his teeth was long extinguished but the notorious gunman continued chewing it as his men brought the four saddled horses through the windswept alley towards him. Fred Smith had not moved an inch since Blake had ordered Weaver and Franks to bring their mounts. He remained at Blake's side, agreeing with every word that came from mouth.

'What you need four horses for, Hoop?' Smith asked. 'I hope you don't think that I'm going with you boys?'

Hooper Blake laughed as Weaver handed the reins to him.

'Bronson needs his horse later, Fred. Once we've taken the wagon to our secret hiding-place and stashed the gold chests, we'll ride back here like nothin' has happened.'

'What about my wagon and team?' Smith asked.

'We'll leave it out near the river.' Blake nodded.

'You can get one of your boys to go fetch it tomorrow.'

Smith nodded in agreement.

'That makes sense. I don't reckon it'd look too good for you boys to bring back my wagon after Harper lit out on it heading for Texas.'

Hooper Blake grabbed the mane of his mount and threw himself up on to the saddle. He slipped the toes of his pointed boots into the stirrups, then gathered up the reins. He knew that the worst of the storm had now left Tent City in its wake. He gestured to Weaver and Franks. They mounted swiftly.

'I sure hope old Bronson did his job.'

Weaver eased his horse up to the side of the thoughtful Blake and tied the reins of Bronson's mount to his saddle fender.

'There ain't no better man at killing than Bronson, Hoop. You know that. He'd kill himself if the price was right.'

Franks laughed as he tapped his spurs into the sides of the horse beneath him.

'C'mon, Hoop. I wanna get this over with.'

'Franks is right.' Blake finally discarded the cigar. 'The sooner we head on out and catch up with the wagon, the sooner we'll be able to come back and celebrate.'

'If Harper ain't dead, things could get messy,' Fred Smith offered.

Hooper Blake totally ignored Smith's cautious words. He slapped his reins across the neck of his mount and drove his spurs into his horse's flesh.

'Let's go get us some gold, boys!' Blake drawled as Weaver copied his actions.

Fred Smith watched the three riders canter away, then entered the rear door of the Angel. The three gunmen were headed out on the same route that they had watched Slim Harper take less than two hours earlier. The sky was still flashing with the remants of the vicious storm that had crossed the valley. Now it was moving over the Black Hills behind them, but none of the riders seemed to care or notice. All they could think about was the three chests of golden nuggets that Harper had taken with him.

Nuggets which they knew would be theirs before dawn.

Kid Palomino and Red Rivers had fought their way through the raging storm to eventually arrive in Tent City. Neither rider had ever seen another settlement quite like the one which they rode into.

The aftermath of the storm had left a lot of damage to the temporary structures but neither horseman seemed to notice as they guided their weary mounts into the dark muddy streets. All the Kid and Red wanted to do was locate the Angel Hotel.

The two bedraggled horsemen drew back on their reins and studied the hundreds of tents which made up the strange mining-settlement. The severe wind had ripped half of the canvas from the wooden frames and frantic miners were hastily trying to repair the unexpected damage.

'Half the street lanterns have gone, Kid!' Red noted.

'Yep,' the Kid agreed.

Palomino stood in his stirrups, looked all around and searched for the Angel Hotel. With few lanterns and torches still alight, it was not an easy task. Then he saw the large wooden building. He spurred his mount and headed towards it.

'Is that the hotel, Kid?' Red asked as he drew level with Palomino.

Palomino looked at his pal and shrugged.

'Who knows?'

The two horsemen made their way through the muddy streets until they were close enough to read the painted side wall. It came as a surprise to both of them.

'Saloon!' Red read the word aloud.

Kid Palomino swiftly dismounted, led his horse to the hitching rail and looped the reins around it. He tied a firm knot in the reins, then flipped the safety loops off his gun hammers. He stepped into the light which bathed the entire area around them.

'You thirsty?' Kid Palomino asked as he stared up into the busy building.

Red slid off his saddle, quickly tied his reins to the pole and moved to the side of his friend.

'I'm always thirsty, Kid. You knows that.'

The Kid half-smiled as he watched men wandering up the street relighting the lanterns which had been extinguished by the savage storm.

'Make sure you got your guns primed, Red. This town ain't got no law and it looks like it don't want our sort within a hundred miles of it.'

'That's why I ain't wearing my tin star,' Red replied.

Kid Palomino unpinned his own deputy's star, removed it from his shirt and slipped it into his pants pocket.

'Good idea, *amigo*. We don't want to give anyone a target to aim at, do we?'

Red followed Palomino up the wooden steps and into the busy saloon bathed in the orange light of smoking lanterns. Both men were surprised at the amount of people within its four walls. But this was the one solid structure within the boundaries of Tent City and the only place where the people felt that they might survive the unexpected storm that had struck without warning.

Now that the worst of the storm had subsided, drunken men were filtering back out of the saloon to discover whether their tents were where they had left them.

'Cover my back, Red,' Palomino whispered as he started across the crowded room towards the long bar. He need not have said a word to the experienced Red Rivers. For more than five years, the older deputy had become an expert at doing just that.

'What'll it be, strangers?' the bartender shouted over the noise of miners enjoying themselves when the two lawmen eventually managed to push their way to the long wooden bar.

'Two beers,' the Kid replied.

The bartender leaned across the wet bar surface.

'We only sell hard liquor in here. You want whiskey?'

Palomino nodded.

'Yep. Two whiskeys will do just fine.'

Red pushed against his friend. He had been studying the crowded room.

'As far as I can tell, there ain't no wanted men in here, Kid,' he whispered.

The Kid accepted the two glasses and dropped a coin into the bartender's hand.

'Where's the Angel Hotel, barkeep?'

'Down the street aways, stranger,' the bartender replied, pointing a finger in the rough direction. 'It ain't much of a hotel though. More like a lot of tents all laced together.'

Palomino raised the glass.

'Much obliged.'

Red lifted his drink, tossed it into his mouth and swallowed. He then shook his head and coughed as it burned its way down into his stomach. He blinked hard and stopped his partner from tasting the potent liquor.

'It's darn rough stuff, Kid. I'd not bother to drink it if I was you.'

Palomino raised an eyebrow.

'No?'

'No! That stuff could strip the paint off a door, boy.'

'You mean that I'd not cotton to it?'

'It could ruin a child of your age, Kid,' Red insisted.

The Kid placed the glass back on the bar and smiled when Red picked it up and downed its contents in one quick motion. The older man kicked the brass footrail and then shook his head.

'Poison, Kid. That stuff's nothin' but poison.'

'Reckon I wouldn't have liked it, huh?' Kid Palomino said as he started towards the swing doors of the saloon.

'Nope. You sure wouldn't have.'

'C'mon, Red,' Palomino said as he moved away.

The two men walked through the crowded saloon and out into the dark street. Kid Palomino rubbed the fingers of his left hand down his face thoughtfully.

'The bartender pointed in that direction?'

'As far as I can figure.' Red followed the Kid down to street-level. Both men mounted and turned their horses away from the saloon. They allowed the horses to walk through the deep mud across the wide street.

'Let's go take us a look,' Kid Palomino suggested.

The two horses walked through the mud as their masters surveyed the array of tents all around them.

Then Red spotted something. He raised his left arm and aimed a finger.

'Over there. See it?'

'Yep. I see it.' The Kid tapped his spurs against the side of his horse and steered the stallion towards the series of tents which boasted of being the Angel

Hotel. The storm had caused quite a bit of damage to the canvas roofs. Stray chunks of the heavy material flapped in the breeze.

'Ain't much like no hotel I ever done seen, Kid,' Red said as he pulled back on his reins.

The Kid rested the palm of his left hand on the silver saddle horn and then slowly dismounted. His every thought was now on Slim and the message he had sent.

'Remember to keep them guns of yours handy, Red,' Palomino said again. 'We might bump into the varmints who have been troubling Slim.'

Red slid off his quarter horse.

'I'm ready.'

The two deputies walked through the damaged frontage of the hotel and stared around its odd interior. They looked at the desk and then down into the maze of narrow gaps that passed for corridors between the rooms.

Kid Palomino walked up to the desk, grabbed hold of the hotel ledger and turned it around until he could read the entries on its neat pages.

Red stepped closer and watched as the Kid ran a finger down the names until he found the one he sought.

'Slim Harper!' Palomino said aloud. 'Room six.'

Red Rivers rested his wrists on the grips of his guns and walked down the corridor staring at the numbers painted on the doors.

'Here it is, Kid!'

Palomino marched quickly to the side of the older

110

man. He tried the handle of the door and was surprised when it opened. They entered and stared at the sparse decoration. The Kid rubbed his chin and then turned to face his partner.

'If Slim was here, he's gone.'

'Gone where, Kid?'

'I don't know.' Palomino walked back out of the room. 'The ledger has no indication that Slim checked out. It don't figure.'

Red slipped one of his guns from its holster and aimed it in the direction from where he could hear approaching footsteps.

'We got company, Palomino.'

The Kid raised a hand to calm his friend and stepped forward to greet the man who was heading towards them.

Fred Smith turned the canvas corner and stopped dead in his tracks. He glanced at the open door to Slim's room and then at the gun in Red's hand.

'What's going on here? Who are you?'

'My name's Kid Palomino, *amigo*. Who the hell are you?'

Fred Smith cleared his throat.

'I own this hotel. My name's Smith. Fred Smith.'

Red spat at the feet of the hotelier.

'Sounds like an alias to me, Palomino.'

'It sure does, Red,' the Kid agreed.

Smith raised both his hands. They were soft like a baby's.

'My name is Fred Smith. Honestly.'

'Where's Slim Harper?' the Kid asked, grabbing

the collar of the sweating man. 'Answer me. Where's Slim?'

'Are you the famous Kid Palomino? The Texan lawman?' Smith asked feebly.

'Yep! I'm Kid Palomino the lawman with a real short fuse.'

'Harper left.'

'When?'

'About two hours back.'

Red cocked the hammer of his Colt and aimed it at the head of the terrified Smith.

'He's lying. According to him, Slim up and left at the height of the storm. That don't make no sense.'

Kid Palomino nodded slowly. His eyes burned into Smith.

'Yeah, it don't make no sense, Red.'

Fred Smith dropped on to his knees and clasped his hands together as if in prayer.

'I swear to you that it's the truth. He bought a wagon and team off me and lit out. He was scared of hanging around in case Hooper Blake and his cronies got him and and his gold.'

Kid Palomino bit his lower lip. Then he hauled the sweating Smith back on to his feet.

'Hooper Blake? I've heard of him. Where is Blake now?'

'They waited for the storm to ease up and then began to trail the wagon, Mr Palomino.'

'How long ago since they rode out?' Kid Palomino screamed angrily into the Smith's face.

'Not long,' Smith gasped in terror. 'I figure it can't

be no more than forty minutes.'

Palomino grabbed the lapels of Smith's coat and hoisted him off his feet.

'You're gonna show us which way they went. Ain't you.'

'You bet!' Smith croaked.

THIRTEEN

The trio of riders sat astride their lathered-up mounts and watched the activities a few hundred yards ahead of them with a mixture of interest and curiosity. The sprawling Tent City was probably one of the wealthiest places within a hundred square miles. Johnny Reno had heard of it, but until now had thought it was just another tale created in the fertile imaginations of drifters. Now he was staring straight at it with eager eyes.

It began to dawn on the notorious gambler why Kid Palomino had been lured here, and to forgo the price on his and his men's heads.

Reno was a man who judged all others by his own standards and all he could see was that Tent City was overflowing with gold. That had to be why the lawmen had come to this place, he thought. They were going to use the law to steal other men's hard-earned fortunes.

For that was what he would do!

Johnny Reno had trailed Kid Palomino and Red

115

Rivers through hostile lands and had already lost two of his men at the hands of an angry Sioux war party.

Now he was sitting with eyes glued to the vast settlement of prospecting miners. He could hardly prevent himself from drooling.

Joe Walker took a mouthful of water from his canteen and then spat the storm from his parched mouth.

'What in tarnation is this place, Reno?'

'Tent City!' came the fast reply.

Davis looked at both his companions. Even in the faint illumination of Tent City's torchlight, he could make out their eager expressions.

'Tent City? What kinda name is that?'

Reno checked his Remingtons, then turned his head to face his hired gun.

'The place that sprang up to let the gold-miners steal all that Indian gold.'

Davis said: 'So that's why we was attacked by them Sioux?'

'Yep!' Reno nodded. He tapped his spurs against the raw flesh of his mount and allowed it to continue walking towards the mysterious settlement.

Davis urged his mount to catch up with Reno.

'How come the Sioux ain't wiped these *hombres* out?'

Reno pointed to the north of the sea of tents.

'The cavalry! They're here to make sure that the Indians don't try nothin'.'

The three riders' mounts gathered pace as they closed in on the conglomeration of canvas tents.

They were being drawn to Tent City like moths to a flame.

'But why did the lawmen come here?' Walker shouted across the distance between them.

Johnny Reno held his reins firmly in his gloved hands.

'Kid Palomino and his buddy are here for a darn good reason, Joe.'

'What kinda reason?' Davis called out.

'Gold!' Johnny Reno answered loudly. 'Them lawmen are gonna steal some varmint's gold.'

Walker scratched the nape of his neck.

'Why would lawmen steal?'

Reno gave out a huge belly laugh.

'They ain't no better than the rest of us, boys. Maybe even a tad worse.'

Kid Palomino and Red Rivers had fed and watered their horses at the rear of the Angel Hotel whilst the terrified Fred Smith had continued to shake. He had no knowledge of either lawman and feared that they just might decide to kill him on the spot to teach him a lesson. Fred Smith had seen many other so-called upholders of the law during his years out in the territories and knew that most men who wore tin stars would shoot first and think later.

He had no reason to think that the Kid and Red were any different from those brutal men.

'Easy, Nugget.' The Kid ran a gloved hand down the palomino stallion's neck as if trying to beg forgiveness for not allowing the creature to rest

117

before expecting it to head out once again on another brutal ride.

'Ready, Kid?' Red asked the thoughtful deputy.

Kid Palomino nodded. He held on to his saddle horn and hopped up until his left boot found the stirrup. When seated on the broad Texan saddle, the Kid pointed a finger down at the hotel owner.

'I ain't too sure what your part in all this has been, Smith. But I give you fair warning that if we discover that you are in league with Hooper Blake, I'll be back.'

Red Rivers mounted his quarter horse and turned its head to face the flat range. Darkness still prevailed. A haunting darkness that he knew offered little cover from their unseen enemies. He glanced down at the sweating hotelier and then tapped the grip of the gun on his right hip.

'And if you are in cahoots with Blake, and something has happened to the Kid's pal, I'll come back and kill you myself. Make no doubt about that, Smith.'

'C'mon, Red. We've already wasted enough time. We gotta find Slim.' Kid Palomino could still see the tracks of the wagon's wheels in the soft mud. He gritted his teeth, stood in his stirrups and then allowed the tall stallion its head. The animal cantered forward with the buckskin quarter horse at its side.

Fred Smith swallowed hard and watched the two deputies heading off into the black storm-ravaged range. The owner of the Angel Hotel suddenly began to feel that the two bags of gold he had tricked Slim Harper into paying him might just have been a small price to be paid for his own life.

FOURTEEN

Defiant shafts of lightning still traced their way across the dark sky above Hooper Blake and his two outriders, yet the ferocity of the raging storm had long since abated. Blake and his men had followed the trail left by the wagon-ruts through the soft muddy ground, knowing that if Bronson had obeyed his instructions to the letter Slim Harper would now be dead. Blake had total faith in the ruthless killing abilities of the large, quiet Bronson.

Starlight now cast its faint light over the flat terrain as the black clouds continued on their destructive journey north above the Black Hills.

Hooper Blake was first to spot their goal.

The sight of the wagon ahead of them bathed in the light of countless stars caused the ruthless horseman to raise his right arm. All three reined in hard and stared into the strange half-light. It was an eerie sight that greeted their attention.

The horses stopped a mere hundred feet from the tailgate of the stationary vehicle.

But Blake sensed that something was very wrong.

The sound of the two harnessed horses chilled all three riders as they vainly tried to break free of their bonds.

Hooper Blake drew one of his guns from its holster and trained it on the wagon.

'Where's Bronson?'

The pair of men to either side of him eased their mounts forward and tried to focus on the motionless wagon. It did seem odd that their partner in crime was not sitting in plain view waiting to be praised for his deadly handiwork.

'Maybe he'd taking a nap, Hoop,' Weaver suggested.

'Maybe Slim Harper was harder to kill than any of us thought,' Blake added.

Franks pulled out his Winchester from its saddle scabbard and cranked its mechanism.

'Cover me, Hoop. I'll take a look.'

Blake and Weaver sat silently on their horses as the cautious Franks threw his right leg over his horse's head and slid to the ground, his rifle gripped firmly in his hands.

Both mounted men watched as Franks made his way across the muddy ground towards the wagon.

'You there, Bronson?' Franks called out. The team of horses moved nervously in their traces but the brake held firmly.

Hooper Blake nodded to Weaver and then allowed his own mount to move slowly behind the walking gunman. The two riders kept their cocked guns aimed at the flatbed of the wagon.

'Where is he, Hoop?' Weaver whispered desperately to his anxious boss.

'Hush up,' Blake ordered.

Franks raised the rifle from hip-height to his shoulder. He closed one eye and looked down the length of its long barrel.

'Bronson!' he shouted again, 'if you're there, I'd sure appreciate you letting us know.'

There was still no reply. Franks turned his head and looked at Blake. He was totally confused.

'What'll I do?'

Hooper Blake dismounted and spoke quietly to the troubled rifleman.

'Stay there, Franks. I'm gonna take me a look.'

Franks continued to squint down the barrel of the Winchester and waited until Hooper Blake was at his side.

'This ain't good, Hoop,' Franks muttered under his breath.

'Damn right it ain't.' Blake moved ahead of the younger man until he was at the back of the high vehicle. He looked back at his two comrades. Weaver was holding the reins of all their mounts whilst Franks was giving him cover. Blake signalled to both men and then slowly began to move around to the large right wheel. He poked the pointed toe of his left boot in the spokes and pulled himself up until he could look into the flatbed.

At first the darkness made it difficult to see anything. Then he noticed the tarpaulin. As his eyes adjusted, Blake could see the unmistakable marks of blood covering the heavy canvas. He continued climbing until he was able to step into the belly of the flatbed.

'What's wrong, Hoop?' Franks asked tentatively as he looked up at his boss's troubled face.

Blake did not reply. He walked up toward the driver's seat and then bent down to lift the heavy tarp. His face lit up when he saw that the trio of wooden chests were still there. Then his cold eyes followed the trail of blood until he was looking down over the two skittish horses tethered in between the traces.

The body of Slim Harper was still lying lifelessly across the wooden poles which separated the black horses, the bullet holes in his jacket stained with blood and black powder from Bronson's pistol.

'I found Harper.' Blake chuckled. He jumped down to the ground beside Franks. He signalled for Weaver to join them with their saddle horses.

Franks edged his way to the front of the wagon and sneered at the sight of the dead gold-miner.

'Bronson killed him good, Hoop. Real good.'

'Damn right!' Blake agreed. 'But where is the idiot? I told him to wait in the wagon until we showed up.'

Franks touched the sleeve of the older man and pointed at something ahead of them on the muddy ground.

'Look, Hoop! What is it?'

Hooper Blake screwed up his eyes and stared ahead of the wagon's team. There was something roughly fifty feet ahead of them on the churned-up soil. Silently, he began to walk towards the object.

'What you seen, Hoop?' Weaver asked as he reached Franks and dismounted.

Blake carried on walking and then stopped suddenly. His gasp echoed all around the open range.

Weaver recognized that his boss had seen something which shocked him. He ran to the side of the hovering gunman.

'What is it?' Weaver asked as he steadied himself on the soft ground next to the tall gunfighter. Then his own eyes gave him the answer that the stunned Blake could not put into words.

'It's Bronson!'

'Yeah. And he's as dead as Harper!' Blake sighed.

The body of Bronson lay curled up on the still soft mud. At least a half-dozen arrows were jutting out from the body like skewers.

Weaver stammered. 'Injuns! Bronson done got himself killed by Injuns, Hoop!'

Hooper Blake looked all around them feverishly.

'I know!'

Franks ran to the gruesome sight.

'Oh my sweet Lord!'

Blake ran his tongue over his dry lips.

'We got ourselves a problem here, boys.'

'What we gonna do?' Franks squealed.

Hooper Blake felt a cold shiver run the length of his spine as he tried desperately to think. They had the gold that they had wanted but now they also had unwelcome company.

'Tie two of the horses to the tailgate, Franks,' Hooper Blake ordered as he led the two men back towards the waiting wagon. 'You can drive it to the hideout. Me and Weaver will ride guard.'

Weaver grabbed hold of Slim Harper's body and hauled it off the wooden traces and tossed it to one side.

'I'll be honest with you, Hoop. I don't like this. I figure we ought to leave the gold and the wagon and ride back to Tent City as fast as we can.'

Hooper Blake shook his head.

'You heard my orders, Weaver. We're taking this gold to the hideout like we planned. I figure the Indians who killed Bronson were just a few strays that the cavalry failed to run off. They're probably a dozen miles from here by now.'

'Or they could be a couple of hundred yards from here watching our every move, Hoop,' Weaver said. 'That's the trouble with Injuns. They're damn good at blending into the scenery.'

'You heard my orders,' Blake growled.

'I heard 'em OK,' Weaver spat as he grabbed the reins of his mount.

Franks secured two of the horses to the tailgate and then climbed up on to the high driver's seat. He knew that he was an easy target and was scared.

'Quit talkin', boys. Let's get out of here.'

Weaver and Blake mounted their horses and began to escort the wagon in the direction of their hideout in the foothills. The flat range was still eerily dark and the three men knew that their every action was probably being watched.

Instinctively they increased their pace.

FIFTEEN

The two horses thundered across the sodden ground following the trail left by Blake and his men and the deep wheel-ruts of Slim Harper's wagon. The sun was rising and a reddish glow swept above the heads of Kid Palomino and Red Rivers as they eventually hauled in their reins and stopped their exhausted mounts.

The Kid removed his jacket and attached it to his bedroll behind the saddle cantle. The dried blood on his left shoulder stained a large area of the blue shirt. Yet he had no time to fret over the pain that still burned into his soul. He was on a mission to help Slim Harper.

Nothing else mattered.

Red unbuttoned his coat, then reached down and plucked a canteen from the saddle horn. He unscrewed its stopper.

'I'm as dry as a . . .'

Kid Palomino looked down at his friend and wondered why the whiskered man had suddenly stopped talking. The expression on Red's face answered the question. The Kid looked to where his pal was staring open mouthed.

The morning sunshine revealed a gruesome sight.

The two bodies lay a mere fifty feet apart but they were both equally dead. Flies had already discovered them and were making their discovery heard.

The Kid teased his reins.

'Forward, Nugget.'

The palomino stallion walked to the first of the bodies and then stopped. The Kid slid from his saddle and stood above the crumpled body for a few seconds as Red Rivers drew level.

The Kid knelt, turned the body over and looked at the muddy face. He wiped the mud from the lifeless features and then lowered his head.

Red leaned over in his saddle.

'Is that Slim, Palomino?'

The younger lawman stood and accepted the canteen from his partner. He drank before returning it.

'Yep. That's Slim OK.'

Red took a quick drink and then hung his canteen back on the saddle horn. He had never seen the handsome face so visibly drained of colour before.

'Look at the other body. It's full of arrows.'

Kid Palomino turned and stared at the corpse of Bronson. Silently he walked towards it. Red trailed his friend atop the buckskin quarter horse.

Palomino bent over. He snatched an arrow from the body and studied it carefully.

'I ain't seen feathered flights like this before.'

Red leaned toward his pal.

'Sioux!'

'You sure?'

'Yep. I had me an incident with them critters about twenty years back.' Red nodded. 'I ain't likely to forget them in a hurry.'

Palomino looked again at the body of Slim Harper and then gritted his teeth as he discarded the arrow angrily. He knew that the man at his feet must have killed the gold-miner before the Sioux destroyed him.

'Easy, Kid,' Red said. 'You gotta keep calm.'

'Nope. I don't feel like keepin' calm, *amigo*. I feel like killing Hooper Blake and his riders.'

'Are we gonna bury Slim?' Red asked.

'Nope. We have to catch his murderers first. When that's settled, we'll come back and take him back to Tent City and buy him a coffin.'

Red watched as his pal whistled to the palomino stallion. The tall horse came to him like a hound returning with a stick.

'Them Sioux didn't mean to kill Slim or this vermin, boy. This is some kinda holy place for the Sioux and they're a tad angry at being evicted.'

Kid Palomino remounted and turned his horse.

'The Sioux didn't kill Slim. His chest is full of bullet holes from a Colt. That varmint killed Slim, not the Indians.'

Red stared at the muddy ground near Bronson's body.

131

'Look, Kid. Unshod tracks.'

'Meaning the Sioux had ponies with them. I already figured that they weren't on foot, Red.' Palomino sighed heavily.

'But did you figure that they're following the wagon?' Red added. 'Coz they are, boy. They're trailing Blake.'

'Good! I just hope they don't get in my way.' Palomino checked both his guns quickly. 'I don't want to have to kill no innocent Indians.'

Red turned Derby and allowed the horse to walk to the side of the brooding younger deputy.

'What you thinkin' of doing, Kid?'

Palomino pointed at the wheel tracks which led off towards the foothills to the east of Tent City. He knew, by the direction that the killers were taking, that they must be taking the gold ore to a hiding-place before returning to the heart of the settlement. He stared out into the distance and the rolling tree-covered hills ahead of them.

'I'm gonna trail Hooper Blake and his gunmen. Then I'm gonna take pleasure in killing them and get Slim's goods back for his wife and daughter.'

'But why do you have to do this, Kid?'

Kid Palomino continued staring at the distant hills.

'Because there ain't nobody else either willing or able to do it, Red. I have to do this for Slim.'

Red Rivers had only seen the ferocity in his pal a few times before but it still scared him. Anyone as skilled with the matched Colts in his holsters was truly dangerous when riled.

And Kid Palomino was riled.

'We can't go takin' the law into our own hands, Kid,' Red protested. 'You and me are lawmen. We have to follow rules. Think about it for a while.'

'I'm done thinking, Red. Now it's time for a show-down.'

'But this ain't right.'

The Kid pointed at the dead body of Slim.

'No, Red. That ain't right. That ain't right at all.' Red's horse reared up as his friend spurred the palomino stallion into action and galloped off after Blake and his followers. He settled the buckskin mount down and then set out after the furious Kid Palomino.

Red knew that he had to catch up with his friend before the Kid did something he would eternally regret.

SIXTEEN

Nature had done a good job at disguising the entrance to the large cave. It was set at the foot of the tree-covered hills which were situated a dozen miles from the array of miners' claims to the east of Tent City. Few of the gold-miners ever ventured anywhere near this remote place for fear of running into the displaced Sioux hunting parties that roamed unseen by the cavalry patrols through the vast forest.

For months since the cavalry had invaded the Indian lands the Sioux had found themselves nothing more than targets for the huge array of weaponry the white settlers and their protectors had brought with them. No one had kept a tally of the exact numbers of Indians who had so far fallen victim to the army's and miners' guns, no one except the Sioux themselves.

It was no wonder that the Sioux were angry and totally confused. The treaty had been broken and yet there was no one whom they could turn to in order to gain justice. Small hunting parties wandered around the hills which overlooked the sea of canvas tents waiting for any opportunity to disobey their elders and seek revenge.

But Blake and his two henchmen had never been frightened by stories of bands of Indians. To the ruthless killers the Sioux were just men, and men could be easily dealt with when you lived your lives by the gun.

Hooper Blake and his followers had discovered the well-camouflaged cave by accident a month earlier when they had brought another of their hapless victims to this remote spot to be executed for not paying them a share of his gold.

Blake had been quick to realize that this was an ideal place for them to hide the vast fortune they were accumulating at the expense of the hard-working prospectors they preyed upon in Tent City.

The temperature was rising in more ways than one and Blake knew it. During the hours of darkness he had sensed that the Indian braves who had killed Bronson were trailing them at a discreet distance. He had not mentioned his fears to either Franks or Weaver for fear that they would panic and leave him to bring Slim Harper's gold here alone.

The bloodthirsty killer had also wondered whether he had been allowing his imagination to run unchecked. But as Weaver and Franks dragged the last of the heavy chests off the back of the wagon and carried it towards the cave, Blake suddenly noticed something on the high ridge above them.

He narrowed his eyes and stared hard into the

trees and dense undergrowth which covered the entire side of the hill. Blake felt sweat trickle down the side of his face. Something had moved across the ridge, but what?

Blake rested his hands on the grips of his guns. His mind raced. Was it animals, or something more deadly? The question burned into his craw unanswered.

For no matter how hard he tried, he could not see anything up there except moving branches.

If it were Sioux warriors, they had yet to attack.

Why?

Hooper Blake knew that the Indians had good reason to pick on him and his men. For it was only a matter of weeks since Blake and his gunmen had run into a five-man Sioux hunting party and killed three of the braves without warning or reason. Perhaps the two Indians who had escaped their deadly bullets that day had returned to seek vengeance on Blake and his confederates.

Hooper Blake saw another fleeting movement on the ridge and felt the hairs on the nape of his neck tingle. He lowered his head and then followed Weaver and Franks into the mouth of the cave before drawing both his guns.

'Drop that box, boys. I reckon we got company!' Blake said, leaning against the cold rock wall and vainly staring up through the overhanging undergrowth.

'What you mean, Hoop?' Weaver drawled, pulling both his pistols and cocking their hammers.

137

'I think that someone is above the cave,' Blake explained, pointing the barrel of one gun heavenward.

Franks looked angry.

'I told you that we should have headed back to Tent City, Hoop. I left my Winchester over on the driver's seat of the wagon. Darn it!'

Hooper Blake could see nothing through the thick foliage from where he was standing.

'Easy, Franks. I'm trying to listen.'

'Are you sure that there's someone up there, Hoop?' Weaver was leaning as far away from the mouth of the cave as possible without actually stepping back into the sunlight. But he could not see anyone either.

'I'm sure that I saw something moving across the ridge above the cave opening.' Blake shrugged. 'I figured that it might be them Indians that killed Bronson.'

Franks gripped the arm of the older man.

'Say that again, Hoop! You thought we might be being trailed by them Injuns?'

'I could be wrong.' Hooper Blake inhaled deeply.

'You're just skittish, Hoop.' Weaver chuckled. 'I reckon we all are after finding Bronson like that.'

'I knew that we shouldn't have killed them redskins a couple of weeks back!' Franks snapped. 'I told you that it was dumb. I bet you that it's the same bunch. They want our scalps.'

Blake stared straight into Franks's face. He knew that the nervous gunhand was right, but he would never admit it to Franks's face.

'It was the cavalry who upset them Sioux in the first place, Franks. They're looking for revenge!'

Weaver was still looking up at the scrub above them.

'I ain't sure there's anybody up there, boys. It might have been a deer that you saw, Hoop,' he reasoned.

Blake rubbed his face along the back of his left hand.

'I sure hope you're right, Weaver. Coz all our ammunition and water is on our saddle horses.'

Weaver held his guns at hip-level and drew in his belly. He gave both men a wink and then smiled.

'I'm gonna walk to the horses and then take me a hard look up at the ridge above us. If I see any Injuns, I'm gonna start shooting. Cover me!'

Hooper Blake nodded at Weaver.

'You keep close to the trees and if they are up there, they ain't gonna have themselves a target.'

Weaver set off in the direction of the wagon. When he was ten feet away from the cave he turned and squinted up into the trees as he continued walking backwards. He kept his guns trained on the green foliage above the entrance to the cave.

'See anythin'?' Franks yelled out.

'Nope,' Weaver replied, continuing to walk backwards to the wagon and horses. He kept his guns levelled on the ridge in anticipation of his being wrong.

Hooper Blake felt as if a huge weight had been

lifted off his shoulders when he saw Weaver reach the wagon.

'Phew! I was starting to sweat there for a while, Franks.'

'Now can we hightail it out of here?' Franks asked as he began to follow cautiously in Weaver's foot-steps.

'You bet!' Blake grinned. He took a step away from the safety of the cave.

Suddenly, clods of earth hit the top of his Stetson. He removed his hat hat and looked up as even more displaced soil filtered from directly above him.

Franks turned and looked over his shoulder at Blake's face. He smiled at the grim expression etched into its hardened features.

'What the hell's wrong with you, Hoop?'

Blake felt as if his throat was being crushed as he vainly tried to call out a warning to both men. At last he managed to yell at them:

'Take cover! There *is* someone up there!'

It sounded like a hundred bees screaming from their hive as dozens of deadly arrows rained over the distance between the ridge and the wagon.

Weaver began to fire frantically as he managed to side-step the first volley of arrows aimed at him. Then his eyes saw the Sioux braves breaking cover with their bows in their hands. One of their number was crudely firing a pair of Colt. 45s.

They were Bronson's handguns taken from his lifeless body a few hours earlier.

Franks seemed to be glued to the ground half-way

between the wagon and the cave entrance, The sound of arrows and guns being used above him confused the gunman.

Before he realized what was happening, an arrow caught him squarely in the centre of his chest. Franks staggered back until his spine was stopped by a tree. The outlaw somehow managed to raise his guns and squeeze their triggers as three more arrows skewered him firmly to the tree trunk.

Franks made no noise.

His head drooped forward until his chin came to rest on his blood-soaked chest.

'Franks!' Weaver called out.

'He's a goner!' Blake shouted.

Weaver moved to the side of the wagon and continued firing at the Indians. He saw one fall headlong off the ridge and crash heavily on to the hard ground. He then ducked when more lethal projectiles cut through the air straight at him. The sound of the arrows hitting the side of the wagon sounded like war drums.

'Get under the wagon, Weaver,' Blake called out at the top of his voice.

He watched as the terrified gunman obeyed his command without a second's hesitation. The bullets ripped at the ground a few feet from the wheels of the stationary vehicle sending debris over his head.

'What we gonna do, Hoop?' Weaver yelled out.

'Try and get Franks's Winchester and start shooting these varmints,' Blake answered, wondering what his own next move ought to be. He was cornered and knew it was only a matter of time before the Sioux braves descended.

Weaver fired both his guns up into the dense green undergrowth that covered most of the hill above the cave entrance. He remained beneath the wagon on his belly trying to see a clear target to train his guns on but the Indians were on the move.

It would be a lot easier if he had the Winchester, and Weaver knew it, but it was up on the driver's seat high above him. To attempt to reach the rifle was almost suicidal as there was no cover, but the arrows were getting closer and Weaver knew that he was running out of ammunition fast.

Another volley of arrows came at him from several directions at once. The Sioux warriors had spread themselves out. Weaver knew that it was now going to be even harder to pick any of them off.

Hooper Blake had mustered every ounce of his waning courage to make a break for their horses.

Gripping the guns firmly in his hands, he ran out of the mouth of the cave firing blindly to both sides.

Before he had covered ten feet of ground, Blake felt the crippling weight of an Indian landing directly on top of him.

Blake hit the ground hard and felt a burning pain tearing through his side. He smashed his right elbow backwards and felt it connect with the face of the Sioux brave.

Rolling over, Blake fired one of his guns straight into the stunned Indian. Then he saw another of the warriors leaping out of the brush high above him.

He cocked his hammers swiftly and blasted the figure. It landed beside him as he tried to raise himself up off the cold soil. Then he noticed the blood which covered his trouser leg.

Blake looked down at his side and then saw the knife sticking out of his ribs. It had been thrust into him right up to its hilt.

Then he saw the Indian with the guns on the ridge.

The Indian was firing both the weapons wildly. Hooper Blake felt another sharp pain and knew that he had been hit. He buckled and rested on his knees staring at the ground as blood dripped from his wounds on to the soil.

There was a full-throated, whooping war cry which echoed all around the remote hillside. Blake tried to look up as he heard the sound of the remaining Indians charging down towards him.

It was useless.

Blake was still staring at the guns in his hands when the Sioux warriors enveloped him.

Weaver had been watching in disbelief.

He had watched Hooper Blake being hacked to bits before he crawled out from under the belly of the wagon and started to climb up towards the driver's seat.

Weaver was praying that the eyes of their attackers would not stray back in his direction until they had finished with the lifeless carcass of Hooper Blake.

He holstered both his hand guns, plucked the rifle

off the seat and cranked its mechanism.

Then he jumped down and knelt with the rifle in his hands. He brought it up to his shoulder and focused down the long gleaming barrel as his index finger teased the trigger.

'Now try and get me, you varmints!' Weaver cursed.

He was confident that he could keep the Indians at a good distance from him with the extra range of the Winchester. He watched the remaining warriors leave Blake's body and turn in his direction.

'C'mon, boys. I'm ready for you!'

The Indians were like phantoms. They used every inch of cover between them as they slowly moved closer and closer to the kneeling gunman.

Weaver's eyes darted from one Indian to the next. His mind was working out which of their number he would pick off first.

Then the painted Sioux with the guns started to run straight at him, screaming out a blood-chilling war cry.

Weaver gritted his teeth and then curled his finger around the rifle trigger. He squeezed it gently but the hammer fell on an empty magazine. Weaver cranked the rifle again and pulled the trigger once more.

As the running Indian closed in on him, Weaver saw the other braves starting to follow.

Again he squeezed the trigger.

The Winchester was empty.

Weaver tossed the rifle aside and drew both his guns. He tried to cock their hammers.

But it was far too late.

They were upon him.

SEVENTEEN

The sight which greeted Kid Palomino and Red Rivers when they eventually reached the abandoned wagon was something that they had not expected. The Sioux had removed their dead from the blood-stained landscape but left the bodies of Hooper Blake and his two henchmen where they had fallen. The savagery with which the Indians had dispatched the three gunmen told the lawmen that this had been a well-planned attack.

Red had once again been correct.

He had said that the Sioux were tracking the three brutal killers, but neither he nor Kid Palomino had expected to find the horrific evidence of their fight in the blazing morning sunshine.

The Kid had suddenly found that his own vicious temper evaporated when he discovered the corpses. For the first time since he had left the lifeless Slim far behind them, he realized the futility of his own desire for revenge.

Both men had been aware that the Indians had

executed their own special brand of vengeance on the dead men scattered between the cave and the wagon.

The saddle horses of Blake and his men were gone. The Sioux had claimed their prize but left the two black wagon horses in their harnesses between the traces.

Kid Palomino dismounted and looped his reins around the rim of the rear right wheel. He tied the knot securely knowing that even his well-trained stallion would shy away from the scent of death that was all around them.

Red did the same and then strode through the grass to the Kid's side.

'Reckon the Sioux did our job for us, Kid!'

Palomino nodded silently, then walked through the trees up the slope towards the entrance to the cave. The sight of more than eight chests of gold stopped him in his tracks.

'So this is where Hooper Blake stashed his loot,' he muttered.

Red pushed his hat off his sweating brow and gazed in amazement at the hoard of stolen ore. He opened the three chests closest to the mouth of the cave. They were all filled right to the lid.

'How many were Slim's, Kid?'

'I don't know.'

Red scratched his beard.

'How many of them should we take?'

Kid Palomino walked between the others and lifted the lids. Each was filled with nuggets. He knew that there had to be a fortune in these innocent-looking boxes. One that he was going to ensure went to Slim's widow and only child.

'We'll take all of them, Red.'

Red felt his mouth fall open.

'All of them?'

Palomino looked straight into his pal's face.

'All of them!' he repeated.

Red moved to the side of the thoughtful younger man who had been unusually silent since their arrival. He rested a gloved hand on the Kid's back.

'We'd better start moving these boxes, Palomino. Then we can head back to the range and pick up Slim's body. Then we can take him back to Tent City. There has to be someone there in the funeral business who'll tend to him.'

Kid Palomino inhaled deeply.

'OK, partner!'

The two men set to work, dragging each of the heavy wooden chests from the cave, down the blood-stained slope and placing them on to the flatbed of the wagon.

By the time the two deputies reached the place where they had first encountered the two dead bodies, the sky was full of circling vultures. Kid Palomino spurred his mount and fired at the birds in an attempt to keep them off what was left of Slim's body. He dropped from his saddle and ran to the defence of his fallen friend, waiting until Red caught up on the wagon.

149

Red hauled back on his long reins and stopped the team of matched black horses a mere few yards from his troubled pal.

'Them birds sure made a mess here, Kid,' Red observed. He climbed down from the driver's seat and made his way to the rear of the wagon. He pushed his quarter horse out of the way and pulled the pins out of the rusted brackets. Silently he lowered the tailgate, then made his way towards the already stiffening body.

It was a gruesome sight. The vultures had torn at the flesh and clothing of Slim Harper in their frantic bid to gain an unexpected meal out on the desolate range.

'Damn vultures!' Kid Palomino snarled and then cocked his gun hammers. Furiously he fired both guns again and again up at the circling vultures. 'I hate them ugly critters!'

Red had never seen the younger man so visibly upset in all the time he had ridden with him. Without uttering another word, Red knelt and carefully scooped the body up in his strong arms and then lifted it up off the ground.

The bearded man walked with Slim in his arms and carefully rested the body next to the wooden chests on the end of the flatbed. He then dragged the heavy bloodstained tarpaulin over the gruesome remains.

Red lifted and secured the tailgate.

'C'mon, Kid. Let's get out of here.'

Palomino emptied the spent shells from his guns

and replaced them with bullets from his gunbelt. He slid the guns back into his holsters, turned, walked to the nervous stallion and mounted.

Red glanced at what was left of Bronson. The vultures had done a far better job on his worthless carcass, he thought.

'I'm sorry, Red,' Palomino mumbled. He tapped his spurs and headed on in the direction of Tent City.

Red Rivers shook his head. Solemnly he climbed back to the driver's seat and unwrapped the reins from around the brake-pole.

'You're welcome,' Red said under his breath.

He released the brake and slapped the reins across the backs of the team. The wagon rolled after the mounted Kid Palomino.

Johnny Reno had only been in the saloon for three hours but had made more than $2,000 at the poker-table. He watched as both Davis and Joe Walker came down the wide staircase buttoning up their trouser fronts as a couple of less than attractive females draped themselves over the banister and waved at their latest customers. Reno touched the brim of his Stetson to the other card-players, placed the paper money in his wallet and coins in his deep frock-coat pockets and then rose to his feet. He walked towards the long bar where his two hired guns were already waiting.

'Sown them seeds, boys?' Reno smiled as he counted the coins which remained in his hands.

'Damn right!' Davis grunted like a satisfied hog.

Apart from the poker-players and a few other men drinking feverishly near a window, the saloon was almost empty. Reno checked his watch before sliding it back into the pocket of his silk vest.

'How much money you make, Reno?' Walker asked, resting his Cuban-heeled right boot on the brass rail.

'Enough for us to have a bottle of whiskey each,' Reno replied. He dropped a few coins on to the counter surface and signalled to the bartender.

Three bottles were placed before them. They grabbed at the bottlenecks and then headed for a vacant table with a good view of the wide street.

'Where's Kid Palomino?' Davis asked. He pulled the cork from the bottle with his brown teeth and spat it into the sawdust.

Reno smiled.

'The owner of the hotel, named Smith, said that Palomino and his sidekick headed out after some critters led by a dude named Blake.'

'Why?' Walker asked as he eventually managed to pull the cork from the neck of his bottle.

Johnny Reno poured himself a measure of the fiery liquid and downed it swiftly.

'Smith mentioned something about chests of gold!'

Walker and Davis drank quickly as if trying to regain the strength that they had drained upstairs in the arms of the fallen angels.

'So you was right about Palomino, Reno!' Walker grinned. 'He ain't no better than the rest of them other lawmen. He was after some other varmint's gold all the time.'

Reno took another drink, then sat forward in his chair. He pointed through the window in front of them. Davis and Walker turned their heads and grinned as their eyes focused on the image.

'Palomino!' they all seemed to say at the same time.

FINALE

It was mid-afternoon as the wagon rolled into Tent City's main street. The scores of Sioux arrows in its side told a story which chilled even the most hardened of onlookers. Something bad had happened out on the range.

That was obvious. But what?

Countless eyes turned and stared at Red Rivers sitting high on the driver's seat whilst Kid Palomino rode silently a few feet behind the secured tailgate beside his partner's tethered horse.

There was a hushed silence as the wagon continued to roll in the direction of the cavalry section of the settlement.

A mounted cavalry officer led a small six-man patrol towards the wagon and stopped next to the grim-faced Kid Palomino. The Kid acknowledged the salute of the officer.

'What happened here?'

Kid Palomino watched as the young major studied

the arrows embedded in the wooden boards of the wagon's side.

'Hooper Blake led some men out after a gold-miner named Slim Harper. They killed Harper and stole his gold.'

The officer's face grimaced when Palomino leaned into the flatbed of the wagon and raised the end of the heavy tarp. The sight of Slim's decomposing body was more than most men could stomach.

'Is that the gold-miner?'

'Yep. That's Slim.'

'But what are all these arrows?'

The Kid replaced the tarp over the body, then rested his gloved hands on top of the silver saddle horn.

'They run into a bunch of Sioux. Reckon you can imagine the result.'

'Is that the gold-miner's gold?' The officer pointed at the chests.

Palomino nodded as he pulled his silver deputy star from his pocket and pinned it on to his shirt again.

'Yep. I know this man's widow. Me and Red are gonna make sure she gets it.'

The officer sighed.

'There is an assayer's office in the cavalry camp. You can exchange that ore for either paper money, a banker's draft or golden eagles, sir.'

Kid Palomino shook the man's outheld hand, then watched the officer lead his small troop through the long line of tents.

Red released the brake-pole and allowed the wagon to continue on towards the army section of Tent City.

Suddenly the sound of a familiar voice echoed out from the direction of the saloon.

'So you managed to get yourselves a whole wagon full of golden nuggets after all, Palomino,' Johnny Reno was sucking on a freshly lit cigar and grinning broadly.

Kid Palomino swung his stallion around and stared hard at the three men who were making their way down the wooden steps towards them.

'Johnny Reno!'

Reno continued to lead his two associates over the uneven ground towards the two startled lawmen.

'I knew you were up to something, Kid,' Reno said through a haze of cigar smoke.

Palomino dismounted and slapped the rear of his mount. It ran a few yards up the street as Red Rivers looked on from his high vantage point atop the wagon.

'What you mean, Reno?' Palomino asked, squaring up to the three men.

'You're as crooked as we are.' Reno spat. 'I figure that you killed that critter in the back of the wagon just to steal his goods.'

Kid Palomino was furious. He tore his gloves from his hands, threw them down and flexed his fingers above the grips of his matched Colts.

'You're asking for trouble, Reno. Now get going before I lose my temper.'

'Did you back shoot the critter, Kid?' Walker chipped in.

'Bet you did!' Davis grunted, resting the palms of his hands on his holstered guns.

'I wondered why you ignored the bounty on our heads.' Reno dropped the cigar and then stepped on it. 'You had yourselves something far more profitable in mind.'

Kid Palomino narrowed his eyes.

'I would never have hurt Slim Harper.'

'I figure that ain't the truth, Kid,' Reno countered. 'I want that wagon full of gold and you're gonna give it to me. Right?'

'This gold belongs to Slim's widow, Reno!' Palomino growled through gritted teeth. 'If you want it, you'll have to get it over my dead body.'

'We're ready for a showdown, Kid.' Reno grinned.

'So am I!' Palomino nodded.

Johnny Reno signalled for his two men to stand either side of him. They did.

'Hold your horses, boys. I'm part of this show-down.' Red Rivers was climbing down the side of the wagon when Johnny Reno drew one of his Remingtons. He fired and hit the bearded man in the shoulder. Red yelled and then fell into the street.

'Red?' Kid Palomino shouted.

There was no reply.

Before the smoke had cleared from the barrel of Reno's long-barrelled .45, Kid Palomino took a step forward and drew both his Colts. Faster than the blink of an eye, his thumbs hauled back both gun hammers and he squeezed the triggers.

Walker and Davis stepped sideways as they too hauled their weaponry from their holsters.

Bullets blasted at the young deputy.

The wide street lit up as the barrels of every gun exploded into action. Gunsmoke spewed in both directions as the deafening noise erupted.

Reno had both Remingtons in his hands and was firing with a speed and fury few had ever equalled.

Kid Palomino felt the hot lead passing to either side of him as he raised the barrel of the Colt in his left hand and fired.

Reno buckled and then toppled on to his knees. Another of the Kid's deadly bullets hit the gambler in the head. He fell sideways on to the ground.

Joe Walker leapt towards Kid Palomino and fired wildly. Then he was hit dead centre and fell in a heap.

Palomino glanced sideways and saw Red holding his gun in his hand. Smoke was trailing from its barrel.

'Look out, Kid!' Red yelled.

A shot caught the Kid high on his left shoulder. A mere inch from the graze he had suffered up in the high forested mountains. He staggered backwards and felt the large wagon wheel at his back.

Davis was wounded yet still coming at him with his guns blazing. Suddenly a rifle shot echoed around Tent City. Davis was lifted off the ground and landed on top of the motionless Walker.

His eyes closed for the last time as his fingers slowly dropped both guns on to the muddy street.

Both Palomino and Red looked down the street in the direction from which they had heard the shot coming. The cavalry officer handed the single shot Springfield rifle to one of his men and then saluted Kid Palomino again before turning his troop and riding out of the tented city towards the range.

Red crawled to his partner's side and managed to get to his feet. Both men were bleeding but knew that they had only been winged.

'You OK, Red?' Kid Palomino asked as he slid his guns back into their hand-tooled holsters.

'Just a tad skinned,' Red replied looking at the dead men before them. 'And you?'

'Got myself shot in the same darn place as last time.' Kid Palomino forced a smile. 'Let's get this gold to the assayer's office and get a banker's draft for Edith and Sophie. The army ought to be able to arrange for a coffin.'

'We taking Slim back to Cooper's City?'

Kid Palomino nodded.

'Yep. He'd want to buried there, Red.'

Red watched the Kid grab his reins and haul himself gingerly on to the saddle of his mount.

'I ain't never seen you so all-fired up before, Kid. Who was this Slim Harper anyway?'

Kid Palomino glanced down at the tarpaulin in the back of the wagon and shook his head sadly. There were tears in his eyes when he looked back at the bearded man.

'He was my brother, Red. My only brother.'